GREGORY EL HARVEY

JACKSONVILLE

A NOVEL

Books by Gregory El Harvey

JACKSONVILLE

Autobiographical
FACES IN THE SHADOWS

Serial
THE PATTERN OF A SNOWFLAKE
DRAGONS MORE DECENT THAN MEN
DRAGONS IN LOVE
TO DIE IN THE COLDEST WINTER
THE AUTONOMOUS ASSASSINS

This book is a work of fiction. All names, characters, and incidents are products of the author's imagination, and any resemblance they may have to anyone or anything anywhere is purely coincidental. All places are used fictitiously.

Cover painting: *Love on a River* by Gregory El Harvey (www.gregharveygallery.com)

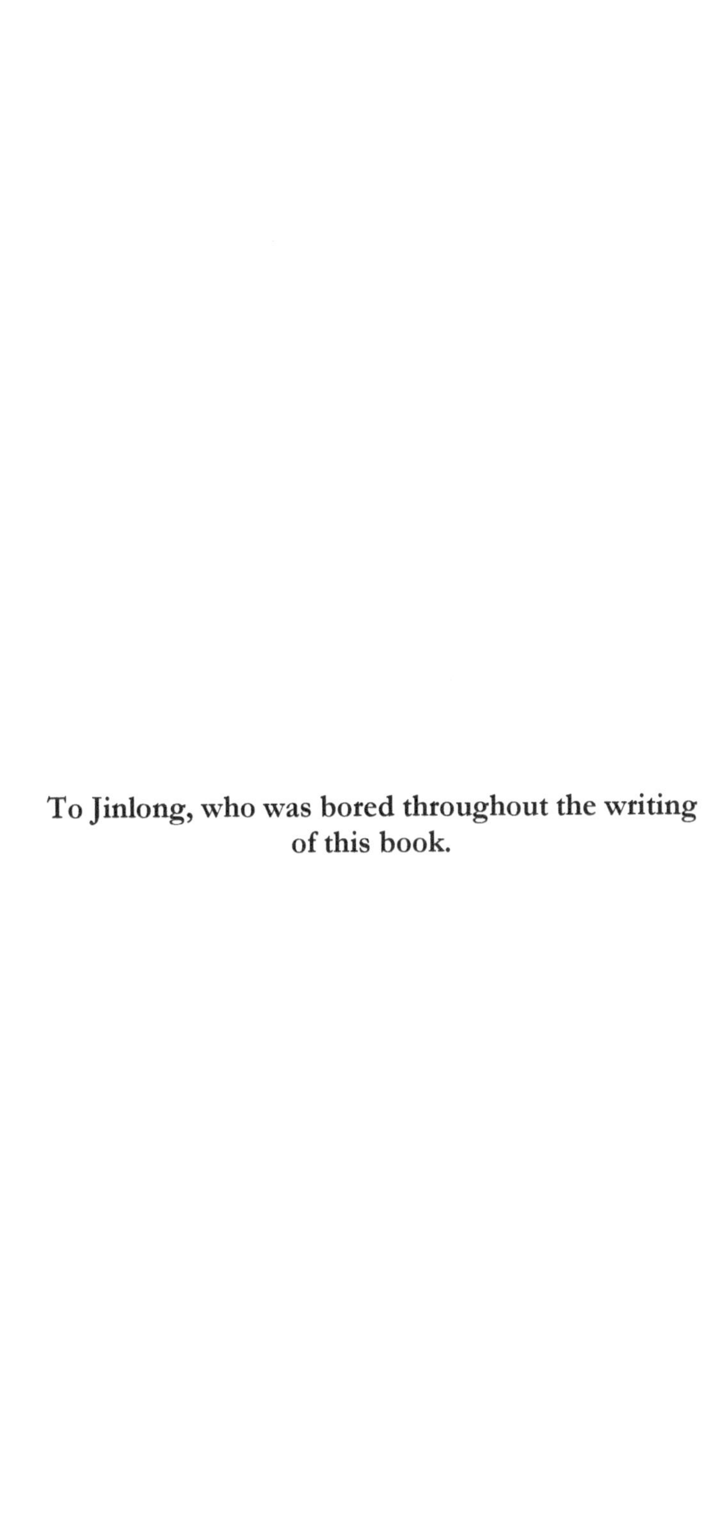

To Jinlong, who was bored throughout the writing
of this book.

ACKNOWLEDGMENTS

I am grateful to Myanna Harvey for critically reading the manuscript and to Cassia Harvey for helping with the publication process.

CHAPTER 1

Summer 1959

"Hi—Terrence?" he said, letting the man in, then closing the door. "Here, have a seat."

"Just Terry, everybody just calls me Terry."

Taking a seat behind the desk, then reaching to give his name plate a nudge forward, "Sure. Terry it is, sure."

For a moment he looked at the man, not merely to appreciate the sheer cruddiness of the sort, but to match, if he could, the man's appearance with what he knew to be true of his character. He let his eyes move over the bright-blue racing car on the lemon-yellow sport shirt. Even across the desk the man's cologne seemed overpowering. He was glad he had not offered his hand. Then he sat back.

"I'm Agent Harold Wright, Terry," he announced. "I'm with the government."

Uneasily the man shifted his position, causing the chair to squeak. "Sure, yeah, hi."

"Is that chair comfortable?"

Hesitantly and with a shrug, "Yeah, it's okay."

"Good." He ran a hand over the top of his crew-cut hair, feeling pleasurably the waxed bristles, then gave his tie a pat. "So, Terry, you're a bad guy, I'm told. Is that so? Don't be shy."

Swallowing, then shifting again, causing the chair to squeak again, "I'm not so bad. I've done stuff, but I'm not so bad."

"Really? Oh, and this conversation is confidential, you can trust me on that. There's nobody here but you and me, so just be frank, okay?"

Hesitantly, "Okay."

"So?"

"Huh?"

"So, are you a bad guy, Terry?"

With a blink, "I'm not so bad."

Wright gave him a short stare. "Well, they tell me just the opposite. In fact, they tell me you're a goddamn killer." And when there was no response, "Tell me about that, Terry—I mean, about being a goddamn killer. What's it like to shoot someone in the head and just walk away? Can you sleep at night? I mean, do you find it easy to shoot somebody? Was it something you had to get used to? I'd just like to get a feel for it, you know, kind of get a sense of it. Tell me what it's like to pull the trigger in somebody's face, let me hear it from a man who knows."

Again the man Terry shifted his position on the chair. Again, the squeak.

Wright again ran the hand over the hair, then brought both hands together. Always such people amazed him, or at least the societal configuration that made such people necessary amazed him.

After waiting in vain for a response, he said with a grin, "Skip it, Terry, I'm just teasing."

Making no attempt to hide his relief, "Oh—sure, yeah. Okay, a joke. Sure."

But then, clearing his throat and putting a little ice in his tone, "You can call me Agent Wright or sir, if you're hunting for words, pal, whichever you like. . . . Let's see, your name is Terrence Dahlmer. And you have a middle name, congratulations, but let's just keep it at Terry. Okay. Let's see," and flipping a folder open, "you're quite a guy. Lot's of convictions, serious stuff. Not just stuff, like you said, but serious stuff. You're a brutal guy, a man of the streets, South Philly streets, to be more precise. You grew up here in Philadelphia, right?"

"Yeah, kind of."

"And I don't think I'm wrong to say you're brutal, since according to this you've been hired to do a lot of brutal things. You're up for a long time, correct?"

"In jail? Yeah, I guess so."

Now the tone was hard. "Look, pal, don't—just don't. I've got your whole criminal history here. You've beaten people up, both men and women. You've stabbed people, and you've shot people. Jail time? Jesus! You know, I don't care what the lawyers got for you, pal—and I *know* what they got for you—I have it firsthand that the authorities are determined that you will never see the light of day again, except from a prison recreation yard. In other words, whatever your misconceptions, you're in for life."

Swallowing hard, then looking toward the floor, "They can do that?"

With a grim chuckle, "Terry, you've killed people. They are, like I said, determined never to let you out of prison. They've got ways, believe me. . . . You're a menace to society."

With a shrug, "Okay, I believe you. Judges are dirtbags. So?"

Wright looked at him, then gave his tie another pat and continued, "Okay, Terry. So, let's talk—no bullshit, okay? You don't lie to me, I don't lie to you. Just the truth, okay? As a government agent—an official government agent, you understand—I need you to do a job. Can you do it?"

A shrug. "Sure, yeah. But how much does the job pay, sir?"

Shaking his head slowly, "Money isn't everything, Terry, at least not to us."

With a look of concern, "But how much?"

"Let's just say, enough to buy you a little freedom."

"How much freedom are we talking about, sir?"

"That depends on how well you do the job, and on how well you behave after the job is done."

"But I would get some money, right?"

"Of course. A man's got to eat. . . . You know, Terry, you shouldn't be focused on your freedom or any payment you might receive. I don't want to go into philosophy here, but relationship is what we're after—the long-term thing, you know?"

The look of concern quickly became one of confusion. "Uh—what're you actually talking about, sir? You want me to blow somebody's brains out, right?"

"Well, blowing someone's brains out is a method for accomplishing a specific, and at this point hypothetical, job. But I'm not talking about that right now, Terry, not about anything specific. I'm talking about a long-term relationship, understand? . . . What I mean is, if you do well with us, we might be able to use you on a regular basis. Would you be interested in that?"

Clearing his throat, "Uh, sure, why not? They said I would have to finish my sentence if I didn't like the deal. And maybe, like what you said, I would never get out of prison. So, I like the deal."

Wright looked at the man, his blank expression, his dull eyes. It was funny how nature could at once produce such different creatures as this man and himself. Could there be a greater contrast? Here was a vicious man, a cruel taker of life—truly a worthless man. And here he himself was, a responsible member of society, with a family and a dog. How could nature make such opposites? It was illogical. In fact, why make this man, this Terrence Dahlmer, at all? And certainly, why ever develop in him such an awful combination of attributes as physical power and a stupid, broken mind?

When the man left, Wright picked up the phone, dialed it, and sat back. He felt good about it all, very good. It wasn't every day that he felt so confident he had done a good job.

"Hello, sir, Wright here."

"How did it go?"

Clearing his throat, "Perfect, sir. I think I can actually describe it that way. He fully agreed. I think we've got our man. And he's a real brute, sir."

"That's good, Bud, but don't count your chickens, okay?"

He felt his jaw tighten. He did not like it when a superior agent assumed the liberty of calling him by his nickname. "No, sir," he replied, giving his tie a pat. "But I think we should at least expect success. I mean, I've been over his file, I've talked to the warden and even the psychiatrist they've got there, and I think we can expect success."

"For this job, would you say, or more?"

"Good question. I guess that will depend on luck. But if everything goes well, I would expect this fellow to be a long-term asset. And I made it especially clear to him that we weren't interested in just getting a job done, but in, uh, utilizing his skills in the long term."

"So, the interview was easy?"

"Well, he did try to play it a little fast and loose, but not for long. As you know, I've been trained to deal with this kind of criminal. I kind of corralled him in by talking to him and forcing him into a corner. It took awhile, but I accomplished it, sir."

"Good. All right, Bud, bring everything to the meeting. But again, this is a sensitive case involving prominent people. So, keep a lid on it."

"Absolutely, sir. I understand the situation. There's nothing actually on paper, and there won't be."

"It's all part of what we do, Bud. It might not be pretty, but it's necessary."

"Yes, sir."

"All right, good job. See you at the meeting."

He returned the receiver, then ran the hand over the hair again.

CHAPTER 2

September

If Shelly Byrne had been born with a different set of gifts, his parents might have expected to prepare him for a career in business or education or medicine or even politics. But when at the age of five both his temperament and his talents were identified by his kindergarten teacher as definitively artistic, his parents began to look for oddities in his personality that might take him in a completely abnormal direction. And when at twelve he spontaneously began to draw and then to paint, no one in the family was surprised. Mrs. Byrne, who had taken the kindergarten teacher's analysis as prophetic, simply smiled at her son's pictures with detached interest, but Mr. Byrne, who as a lawyer was headed into politics, overtly frowned.

As for Shelly, life was what it was, and he was determined to be content with what nature had given him. In high school his art blossomed. He moved from watercolor on paper as his primary medium to oil on canvas. Later, at the Pennsylvania Academy of Fine Art, he simply walked through the philosophical doors as they opened, discovering an entirely new set of rules for the expression of his art.

But during his third and final year at the academy he dropped out and moved to Greenwich Village in New York. There he rented a one-room second-floor apartment and set up his studio. Within six months he found acceptance in a few local galleries. His circle of friends changed. He began to drink more heavily and he met Margot.

Margot Bernard, whose wealthy parents had immigrated to New York City from France in the mid-30's, spent two years at Wellesley before moving to the Village. She was asked to leave the famous college after submitting and subsequently refusing to retract or even apologize for a paper she had written replete with the grossest profanity. Her bifurcated response to this rejection by the corrupted system, as she described it, involved the presentation of her middle finger to the faculty, along with a quick verbal delivery of her philosophy that humans only spoke the truth when they were profane. After turning her back on academia, she moved back to New York and the Village. It was there, in a bar, that she met the artist Shelly Byrne.

It was a scene memorable for both of them, so that later each could recall it precisely, albeit subjectively. The artist simply walked in, and the writer simply looked up. For the writer it was the long, miscreant, reddish-blond hair, the white poncho, the worn jeans, the cowboy boots, and yes, the sensual, nearly feminine walk that were recorded in her mind. For the artist, it was the short, brown, boyish hair, the bangs, the full brown eyes, but especially the rocky muscles that rippled along the forearms.

There were other things, of course, that had turned their meeting into magic. For years Shelly would recall his irresistible attraction to Margot's ability to swear like a sailor yet be sensitive like a saint. Margot, on the other hand, would inevitably recall her attraction to the way Shelly could easily use either the ladies' room or the men's, as if both were the same to him.

"You were born in Rouen," he observed, "but grew up in New York. No wonder you have no distinct accent. Rouen associates you with Joan of Arc, so you must be a deliverer."

It wasn't long before Margot had moved into Shelly's studio and the two were sharing not only the same workspace, but the same bed as well.

"I am twenty-six and you are twenty-seven," said Shelly one evening as they made their way toward a coffee shop and bar, "which means that probably at least one third of our life is already gone."

"Which means what?"

"Which means that now—in the middle third of our life—we should be spending all of our energy on our work."

"I thought," she said, "you were going to say that it meant we should be getting married."

He gave her arm a squeeze. "But that's obvious. At least, when I think about it."

"So, will you marry me?"

"And did you get me a ring?" he returned simply.

"Not yet," she replied, "but maybe I will."

"But I want to say it out loud," he went on, as if returning from a distraction, "so I think about it and deliberately do it."

"It?"

He gave her a look. "The work, of course. Come on, Margie, humor me. It's like sex. I don't want to have to look back on it to appreciate it."

Squeezing his arm again, "So, you think we're too bohemian to care a lot about the work?"

"Maybe."

"Okay--say I agree. So, let's love deliberately and work deliberately, and stop frittering away the middle third of our life in coffee shops and bars. How's that?"

"Now you're humoring me too much."

"All right," she said as they halted at a crosswalk, "how about this? Doing anything too deliberately turns the experience into an intellectual exercise. I want to have a sensuous and sensual life. I want to live life, not just understand it."

Later, over beers, he said, "But we are all intentional creatures. So, what is real?"

"The trick," she replied, overtly flexing the muscles in her forearms, "is to look deeper, past the mask, if someone will let you, and find the soul, the very architecture of it."

Observing the muscles, "And finding the soul is what? Love?"

"Of course."

Moving a handful of hair behind his ear, "But I haven't found your soul, and yet I love you."

Again she flexed the muscles. As she let her eyes move down over his hair she felt her stomach nearly collapse. "When you look into my eyes," she said, "and I let you look into them, you see my soul."

Dropping his voice, "I think you writers are pretty much fucking nuts."

"And you artists are not?"

Momentarily, "I have a question for you. Neither of us takes drugs, yet we both drink. If each of us has found the soul of the other, and thus has found love, why do we drink? Why do we not simply suffice ourselves with each other's love?" And when there was no response, "Come on, Margie, you're the writer, invent an answer. Why do we drink?"

"Alcohol is an intrinsic part of the physical world, part of the earth, like food and sex."

"Cute. And what would you say about painting and writing, art and literature?"

"Painting and writing are like sex. Art and literature are like babies."

"You seem to have sex on the mind."

"I do, Mr. S. Byrne. I do."

"Then why," he came back, following her hair as it had been combed back past her ears, "are we here drinking?"

"I have no idea."

It was at such a bar that they met Sally Boxer Klein, a journalism major, and her boyfriend, Michael DeVal, a political science major, both at Columbia University. The couples were brought together when the bar's space at tables ran out and the evening's messenger began to pick her guitar, then to sing. Scooting over, they invited Michael to take an empty chair and Sally to sit on Margot's lap. When the final song closed and the lights came back up, the couples ordered more drinks and peanuts and talked until it was late.

The next day, the couples met for lunch and beers. Although no one pointed it up, the natural camaraderie was obvious. During the days and weeks following their first meeting, the four found themselves spending more and more time together. Often they would spend an entire evening and much of the night drinking their way through conversation and discussion.

During one such evening, as Margot sliced cheese onto a plate in the studio, Michael argued with Shelly over social rights. When the discussion became heated, as Shelly wanted nothing of Michael's socialistic idealism, Margot cleared her throat loudly, handed the plate of cheese and crackers to Sally, and said, "So, Sally, from the way you've described your childhood, you grew up richer than I was."

"Very possibly."

"Well, she's sure rich now," put in Michael. "Which makes me feel like a dope sometimes. Think of all the people she could be helping to feed."

"Or," returned Sally, "I could just buy tanks for the army, or something like that. How about that, Michael, would that work?"

He grimaced, reaching for a cracker. "Not exactly."

"I don't feed people, Michael. And you don't know that? Typical idealist—head in the goddamn sand! You sleep with me, but you don't know who I am or what I believe."

Somewhat indignantly, "I know who you are, and I know what you believe too."

"But," she added, overtly sarcastically, "you just feel forced by your conscience to point it out all the time that rich people live with unconscionable social disparities."

"Oh, I'm afraid it's worse than that," he shot back. "The rich cause those disparities and then not only live with them but invest in them to keep them going. The rich are simply exploiters, monsters."

Margot pulled the cork from a bottle of Cabernet, then handed it to Sally. "And who are the rich, Michael?" she queried, turning to him. "You yourself are rich, sitting here with friends, eating cheese and drinking wine. Actually you are stinking rich, compared to much of this world you care so much about. And I'm sure you know that."

"Of course I do," he came back, popping another cracker into his mouth.

"But by labeling some people as 'the rich,' you've made it a qualitative thing, when really it's a quantitative thing. People are richer than others, that's all. Everybody's richer than somebody. All you've done is stuck a label on people you think you don't like, when you don't even know who they are or how much wealth they actually have. How rich do my parents, for instance, have to be in order to get plastered with your label? Would an income of a hundred thousand a year be enough?

Two hundred thousand? Do they have to be worth a million, two million?"

"I understand what you're saying, Margot," he returned. "But it wouldn't be that difficult to determine who the rich are. You could just look at their tax statements, for instance, or count the Cadillacs in their driveways."

"And who would decide where the cutoff is? You?"

"Why not? I've got a good head on my shoulders. I care about the poor. There are lots of other people out there who care, too. There could be a committee for making the decision."

"And who would choose the committee members?"

"I think I could do that."

With a shake of her head, "So, you and your committee would decide quantitatively who qualitatively was rich and who was not, and then label them as monsters. And that's not far-fetched, is it, since you just did that a few minutes ago."

He merely looked at her, then took a sip of his wine.

Then Sally leisurely took the bottle up and refreshed her glass. Handing him the bottle, she looked at him for a moment, then said, "So, when you sleep with me you're screwing a monster, is that what you're saying?"

He stared at her, holding the bottle but not pouring himself any more. "That's harsh, Sally."

"You generalized, asshole. And you were pretty quick to do it."

Still he held the bottle and looked at her. "Well, then, I apologize, dear."

With a sigh, "Would you just pour yourself more wine, then, and pass the goddamn bottle?"

He did so, but then did not look at her for the rest of the evening.

"Yes," said Sally to Margot, "my parents are stinking rich, and like Michael said, so am I."

Margot smiled, but not with a happy smile. "Well, I'm not," she said. "My parents didn't like it when I married this goofy cop. But as it turned out, neither did I. He was cute and could even be sweet, but he was also one of the meanest pricks I think I've ever met in my life. Such a bastard he turned out to be! So, I divorced him. . . . When I tried Wellesley, they paid for everything. When I left and moved here, everything stopped, with an exclamation point. Now I see absolutely nothing from them."

Michael looked up from his wine. "Is it developing character in you?"

She shot him a glance. "Hell fucking no."

"My parents," said Shelly, "are pretty well off. I grew up not wanting for a single thing. If I wanted something, which was rare, they simply got it for me. I don't have a head for money—I'm kind of daft about it, as the British would say. They wanted me to go into some kind of profession. But I was really young when I sort of identified with the arts. I was doing serious pictures even as a kid. So, they relented and even seemed a little happy that I was accepted at the academy. They could at least tell people I was in a reputable school. But then I just up and left the school. Not good. They were so disappointed. Anyway, they still send money occasionally, like in a card, but I'm pretty much on my own. My dad wants to be a senator."

Michael put his glass down. "We didn't have much as a family when I was growing up. We weren't dirt poor, but there didn't seem to be an extra dollar to spare, that's for sure. We kind of made everything for Christmas, that kind of thing. My mom even made birthday gifts. There would have been no chance of college for me, if it hadn't been for the scholarship. My parents were really happy about it. Their dream for me, I'm sure, is that I will be rich. But I don't want to be rich. I don't even want to think about money. I don't like money."

"I'd like to say," said Sally, "*but you like to drink wine, don't you?* But I know you, and you truly are so idealistic that you could probably do without wine for the rest of your life, or even a place to sleep, just to make the world better. God! How did we ever get together? We're such opposites."

CHAPTER 3

Perhaps it was the gloom unique to the city of New York that caused everything to shift for Shelly and Margot, or perhaps it was their own inner gloom that did it. A certain melancholy seemed to be creeping into their thinking and their work. They found themselves leaving the studio more frequently than usual and taking to the streets and bars for distraction. But when even the company of Sally and Michael could not suffice to cheer them up, they began to assess less favorably their prospects for working successfully in the Village. And when seemingly at once the galleries began rejecting Shelly's work as not vanguard enough, and the publishers to reject Margot's submissions as from a writer not established enough, they both resolved to leave New York.

So, in search of a warmer climate, a less competitive market for Shelly's painting, and a less frantic atmosphere for Margot's writing, with only three hundred dollars cash between them, they bought an old pickup, loaded it with studio equipment, typewriters, books, and what furniture they could fit, and set out for Florida.

"You left your husband," said Shelly, "and then Wellesley, and I left the academy. We both have a strong spirit of refusal."

"Refusal of what?"

"To be conquered."

"Well, at least you're being positive about it," she replied. "I hope you're right. I think you're right. But if you're wrong, and we really just have a spirit of foolish rebellion, we could be throwing both our careers down a hole. Besides, are we really leaving New York out of refusal, as you say, or because we're just bored?"

"Maybe because of both," he returned. "But when you're bored you can be controlled by people who reward you with little shows here and insignificant publications there. An artist or writer can be destroyed that way. We're refusing to be destroyed by that kind of thing. We're not insisting on success, but we are insisting on survival."

"You sound very courageous."

"No," he replied, "I'm not courageous. I'm too afraid of too many things to be courageous."

"Then what were you saying by all that grand shit stuff just now?"

"Not really anything. Just making excuses."

"Do you think we'll be happy in Florida?"

He looked over at her as she drove. He loved to watch her do things. He had always enjoyed watching people show strength and do difficult things. Finally he answered simply, "No."

In Jacksonville, which they picked from the map on the drive south, they rented an old two-story house, sold the truck, and bought a repossessed 1956 Oldsmobile 98 Holiday sedan. The car had white and charcoal two-tone paint and was equipped with a 240-horsepower Rocket V8 with a 4-barrel carburetor, dual exhaust, and a Hydramatic transmission. Just feeling the power through its accelerator, made Margot's heart pound with excitement as she drove it home from the dealer.

The house, on the corner of Harris and King, lay just half a block down from St. Johns Avenue and one block up from the St. Johns River. The cedar-shingled frame structure was old but sound. Its rooms were spaciously laid out, with a grand living room, a charming dining room, drawing room and kitchen, a beautiful staircase, four second-floor bedrooms, two full bathrooms, and a useable attic. The garage was useable, but had a dirt floor, and the driveway was tiny and gravel covered. Large trees surrounded the house, including two huge and very 'dirty' sycamores. The only serious negative about the property was that the house had a leaky roof.

The neighbors beside them—a man and his wife and three young sons—seemed friendly, but definitely not sociable. The two boys, aged ten and twelve, were very respectful and avoided cutting through the yard. They were very proud of their baby brother, only two years old, sometimes pushing him in a stroller around the next block. The neighbors across the street—a single mother with a teenaged daughter and younger son—

seemed distinctly aloof. The neighbor on the other side of the dirt alley—an older woman—they rarely saw.

An oddity about the location was that along one side of the house ran Harris Street, a short half-block of asphalt that led directly to the emergency room of the St. Vincent Hospital. The big Cadillac ambulances would make their turn at King and Harris, then tear, full throttle, toward the hospital. The first few times it occured, Shelly and Margot found it to be exciting. But since it happened at any given hour of day or night, it soon became merely an alarming annoyance. Margot, with her writing studio located on the second floor and just above the corner where the ambulances made their turn, came to describe the experience as not unlike having a train roar past the house.

But overall the neighborhood was unusually quiet, reflecting the efforts of the hospital, overtly Catholic, to promote a reverential ambience. A general rule of respect for quiet was not only fostered but was often enforced throughout the hospital proper and over its grounds, which, bordering on the St. Johns River, occupied most of the block. Everywhere both men and women religious moved about as they performed their duties or, often in two's, simply strolled the walkways by the pampered lawns. The nuns especially, with their huge coifs, seemed the perfect guardians of this reverential quietude.

"Margot!" yelled Shelly, "can you get that?"
"No, just getting out of the shower!"

The other frantically grabbed a T-shirt and ran downstairs. Lifting the receiver from the wall box, he put it to his ear and said, "Hello, Shelly speaking."

"Mr. Byrne?" came the man's voice.

"Yes."

"Is this the artist Shelly Byrne?"

"Yes."

"And does Miss Bernard live there, too?"

Something in the voice, the tone, the words, made him hesitate. "Yes—yes, she does. Who is this, please?"

"Well, I like art. My name's Terry, and I like art. I like books too."

"Yes?"

"Well, I was wondering if I could come by and look at some paintings that you do."

"And um, how did you hear about my work, can I ask? Was it through the gallery?"

Momentarily, "Yeah. Yeah, it was great. I saw one of your paintings there, and I really liked it. I'd like to see more of your paintings and maybe buy one. When would be a good time to come by and see some art?"

Again he hesitated, but this time because of the sheer pragmatism behind the voice. Surely this person's interests must be very far from art. Finally he offered, "Uh, well, how does Friday sound to you?"

"That sounds good, Mr. Byrne. What time?"

"Oh, say, ten or eleven—in the morning, that is."

"Sure, yeah. I'll be there."

"So—which would be best for you, closer to ten or to eleven?"

"Yeah, okay, maybe ten, sure. And you're on King Street, is that right?"

"Yes. We're on the corner of King and Harris, but facing King."

"What is it, a house?"

"Yes, a two-story with brown shingles. Harris is the street that leads to the hospital, St. Vincent's Hospital. It's Catholic, and you can't miss it."

"Good, sure. I'll see you then, Mr. Byrne. And maybe I can meet Miss Bernard too. I like books too and meeting writers. Will she be there?"

"Uh—she should be, yes."

"Great. And I'll bring money to buy paintings."

With an uneasy shake of his head, "Okay, we'll see you then, uh, Terry."

"Yeah. Goodbye, Mr. Byrne."

"Goodbye."

Following dinner that evening, he put water on for tea, then said, "I don't know why, but it's still bothering me that he asked about you."

She pushed the bangs from her eyes. "And not a reader, huh?"

With a chuckle, "He sounded like he had never read a book in his life. . . . Look, I just don't feel okay about this. I'd be happier if you were here."

"I've got practice at eight and a game at five, and you knew that when you scheduled this."

"I know, I know."

"You sell your art, Shelly, I don't sell my books. Bookstores do that. Why would I have to be here? The practice is important."

"I can't explain it. I just—please, Margie, I'd feel better. Just for when he's here. Please."

Momentarily, "Sure."

On Friday, just after nine, he looked out the kitchen window as he heard the Olds pull in. Although the sound of its tires on the gravel and its engine shutting down always gave him a sense of peace, today it did especially so. But continuing to watch, he could see from the way she slammed the car door that she was annoyed at having to cut the practice short.

Sweaty and with her brow furrowed, she strode into the kitchen, her bat resting on her shoulder. Tossing her glove onto the table, she gave a quick and clearly perfunctory smile, then pulled a chair out and sat.

"Hear anything from him?" she queried.

"No. Sorry."

"Well, should I take a quick shower, or just hold off, in case he comes early?"

"Uh—why don't you hold off. I'd feel better. Besides, you smell really nice."

Clearing her throat, "Okay."

Momentarily, "I know the practice was important, Margie, but I just didn't feel comfortable having him come here with you away."

She met the green eyes. She loved this man. But clearly there was something to what he said. For a moment she let her eyes follow the flowing hair. Finally she replied gently, "It's okay. I understand. I think we both have to be careful. The world's getting crazier. I was thinking, maybe we should get a gun or something. Just for the house. I know you're not afraid of people, but I don't know—just for house protection."

"A gun? Really?"

"Just a small one," she replied. "Just a little one you could put in your pocket. You used to sell paintings out of the studio, and now it looks like you might start selling out of the house. I mean, there is some danger there, I agree. That's your concern, right?"

He ran a hand through his hair. "Yes. . . . Did the coach say anything about your leaving?"

With a shrug, "She frowned, but that's all."

"Did you get to practice hitting?"

"Our cleanup pitcher threw a few for me. But there wasn't anything there, so I just let them go. Then I swung through a couple, but missed them. The coach wasn't happy about it."

"You're her power hitter. I doubt she's worried."

With another shrug, "Well, I always like to get some wood on the ball before a game."

"Sorry, Margie."

"So, do you have the paintings ready to show him?"

CHAPTER 4

At five minutes before ten the doorbell chimed. Shelly dried his hands on a towel, went to the door, and pulled it open to a man of medium height with blond hair and sunglasses, wearing a black sport shirt and tan pants. Even as he had pulled the inner door open he felt uneasy. Now, pushing the screen door open for the man, he noticed a definite pain in his stomach.

"Hi, Terry?" he said cheerily, stepping aside as the other entered.

"Yeah, that's me. Is Shelly Byrne here?"

"I'm Shelly."

The man looked at him. "Oh, I'm sorry. I thought you was the girl."

Pushing the inner door closed, "Yeah, the hair sometimes confuses people. It's fine. Come on in."

After looking him up and down again and grinning, "Sure. I'm here. So, can I see some paintings now? That's why I'm here, just to look at art and buy stuff."

"Certainly."

"Okay, yeah. So, lead the way, uh, sir."

He had determined not to show the studio. He never enjoyed having people look at his things in progress anyway. But especially today, with someone he didn't know and had an uneasy feeling about—well, no. So, he led him to the living room. Selecting a piece from a group of five unframed oils leaning against a wall, he set it upon a portable easel, turned to face the man, and presented an amiable smile.

"This is an abstraction of a landscape. It's oil on linen, 24 by 30 inches, and would frame up nicely in a simple molding. Do you like abstracts, Terry? Or would you like to see something more representational, more realistic? You haven't told me what kind of art you like."

But the man, still grinning and eyeing the long hair, simply stood in the double doorway from the foyer and looked at him. Finally he replied, "Yeah. ... So, where's the writer?"

Hesitating, for now he felt a distinct grip of uneasiness in his stomach, he said, "She plays softball, and I think she might be practicing."

The grin disappeared. "Where?"

It wasn't the question, it was the tone—the demanding tone. The uneasiness turned to a definite fear. With his throat tightening, he did not answer, but simply looked back at the man.

"Where is she?" the man repeated, the tone now cold. "Is she around here? You said she'd be here."

For a moment he continued to look at the man. Then he drew a breath, fixed his eyes on him, and called out, "Margot, could you come here?" And when the man took a step closer, "You know, I think she might be out in the yard practicing ball. We could go out there, if you want." But there was another step, and now he saw it, a black revolver pulled from the back pocket. Fortunately the man stopped about six feet away.

"I don't see her," he said menacingly. "Tell her to come in. Just yell."

"Is this a robbery? I don't have much money, and the paintings aren't worth much, because I'm not well known."

"Call her now," he snarled, "or I'm gonna put a hole in you, fag, or girl, or whatever the fuck you are. Call her."

He looked at the gun, then back at the man's contorted face. Taking a breath, he called out, "Margot! Please!"

Just as the gun was raised to chest level, Margot strode in from the hallway coming from the kitchen. Wearing a ball cap and slinging a bat on her shoulder, she projected a nonchalant air. She did not look at the gun. "Hey there," she said jovially, walking toward him, a light spring in her step, "what's the matter, what's going on?"

As he swung the gun at her to his right, she moved left, turning him more away from Shelly.

He followed her with the gun. "Stop right there, lady," he commanded, his back now to Shelly.

Instantly Shelly stooped, grabbed a half brick he had been using as a curtain weight, and threw it, hitting the man in the back. As he reacted by spinning and firing at Shelly Margot put both hands on the bat and lunged at him. With all her might, she brought the hickory down upon him, striking him in the neck.

As he went face down with a thud upon the old hardwood floor Margot stepped forward, lifted the bat, and brought it down upon his head with a terrific smack. The instrument hit him with such force that its hickory cracked along with his skull. Then frantically she raised the bat and hit him again and again and again and again. Breathing hard, as if she had run the bases all the way to home plate, she stood over him and looked down at his crushed head while slowly the blood began to ooze from it.

"Did he get you, Shelly?" she queried, grasping the bat now in one hand, like a hammer.

"No, I don't think so. God almighty! Jesus! . . . Do you think he'll get up?"

She looked down at him. "Yeah, he might." And bringin the bat over her head, and with both hands again, she brought it down like a maul upon his cheekbone. "Now—I don't think so."

"Goddammit!" Shelly nearly screamed. "Look at him! He was going to kill us!"

Slowly Margot took a step back then laid the bat down. Already a distinct blackish-red pool had formed and was increasing around the man's broken head, and blood was beginning to drip from the garish split on the shattered cheekbone. "Something tells me," she said, with a quick sniff, "he's done. No, the dirty shit's not getting up."

"That's redundant," came back Shelly, staring down at the corpse, "all shit's dirty. A writer should know that."

As if she hadn't heard this, "Right. Listen, I'm going to call the police. Don't step in any of the blood."

Within minutes a scream of sirens and blatting of tailpipes brought a pack of the elite Jacksonville city police motorcycle corps. Sliding in, tires screeching on the pavement and throwing gravel in the driveway, they swarmed into the house and over the property.

As the kitchen door was yanked open and a big cop stepped past him, Shelly stood aside and pointed to toward the hallway. "He's in the living room," he said. "He tried to shoot us."

The six big men, silent and with guns drawn, strode past him and quickly surrounded the fallen man. Standing over the body, they said nothing as one of them put his finger to the man's neck. When he stood the others reholstered and simply walked out, as if disappointed. Within seconds there was a horrific roar as the big Harleys blew away from the property.

The officer who had felt the man's neck looked down at the corpse and the bat, then up at Margot. "You hit him?" he queried, giving her a look up and down.

She gave a single nod. "I did, yes. He fired at Shelly here, and then I swung on him."

"Margot's a hitter," put in Shelly, pushing his hair back, "on the Avondale A's"

"So, did he force his way in?" he asked, his southern accent heavy. "Did he come in with the gun out, or did he pull it later?"

"He pulled it out later. He had called for an appointment to look at my paintings, but drew the gun after he was inside."

"But you don't know him?"

Shelly shook his head. "No. He's was a total stranger, I'm afraid."

Then he simply grinned and ran his eyes up and down Margot. "Well, ma'am," he said to her, taking in the rocky muscles, "this man's dead. You got yourself a homerun, looks like."

"Yeah," she returned, "but I broke my bat."

"Well, you split the floorboard there too, look at that. I think you over reached him there a bit on one swing. That's what probably broke the bat actually." Then looking at Shelly, he said, "It's good he didn't get you with that little popgun there. I mean, it's a real gun—it's a .38, and he'd a-killed you with it. Are you sure he didn't nick you?"

"No—yes—I mean, I'm sure."

"Okay, okay. . . . Well, ladies, he was inside your house, pulled a gun and fired on you, so I don't think you'll have a problem with us. And especially since you just had a bat against a gun. So, I'll call it in and fill out my report. There's got to be body removal and such as that. But it looks to me to be a pretty simple case of self-defense. I don't make the decisions—downtown does that—but I'll put in my report what it looks like."

"Will somebody be out today, I hope?"

With a chuckle, "Yeah, prob'bly. You ladies have got yourselves a mess here. He's gonna stink pretty soon. . . . Man! Look at that head!" And looking down again at the bat, then at the grossly bloodied head, then up at Margot, he grinned and simply uttered, "Jesus!"

When he had gone and they were waiting for more police to come, Shelly said, "He called us 'ladies,' the crazy cop."

"Well, he looked you up and down, like he wanted to take you to bed."

"He looked you up and down, too, girl, you and your goddamn muscles."

"Not like he did you. Man! It's that hair of yours, I think, and those gorgeous green eyes. No wonder everybody thinks you're a girl. You'll have to show him your dick sometime."

CHAPTER 5

Closing the blinds, Wright gave his head a shake. Why did Philadelphia have to be so goddamn gloomy in October? And what was it with people, always saying how beautiful autumn was? He considered it to be a downright shitty time of year. But he couldn't say as much, or the secretaries might get the impression he was unhappy.

Returning to his desk, he sat for a moment. Then, with authority, he shoved the drawer home, picked up the phone and called her back.

"Yeah, it's me. Listen, I'm going to say it once more—I didn't take your shears. And you shouldn't call me at the office like that just to spout off at me about little things. And you know that. . . . I don't care. Don't call me about stupid things. . . . Yeah, I am saying that. You did hear that, I think, right? . . . One more time—I didn't take your shears. . . . But I didn't take them, just get it into your head, that's all. . . . I don't know, Darlene. How could I know, since I didn't take them? Go look out in the yard. You probably left them out there in the rain. Now they're rusty, and we'll have to buy new ones. ... Hey, you don't have to swear at me, Darlene. ... Well, goodbye to you too. ... Goodbye yourself, then. ... All right, goodbye."

Dropping the receiver onto the hook with a kiss-my-ass click, he slumped back in his chair, inserted a finger between his collar and neck, and gave a pull. Why did his neck seem to swell every time she called? Probably because he had come to sense how much she disliked him. She was becoming more and more a pain with every squabble. And clearly she was the one starting the fights.

Then the line came through again, and he picked up. "Agent Harold Wright. ... Yes, John. ... You're kidding. ... You're kidding. ... Damn! ... Oh God, oh God! Damn! How in the hell? ... Well, the stupid guy. What'd they use? ... You're kidding. A softball bat, a goddamn softball bat? You've just got to be kidding. ... Well, what did he have? ... A six-shot .38. Okay, great. A bonafide killer with a gun against a girl from Wellesley with a softball bat. Oh my God! ... Yeah, sure, right— he won't have to go back to prison, very funny. Serves him right. Good Lord! ... Yes, yes, I'll, uh, I'll call, sure. ... Yeah, yeah, I understand. I'll call, don't worry about it. ... I don't know, John, I have no idea frankly. He'll probably buy himself a gun now, and they'll have to rent an army. I don't want anything more to do with this, John, and I'm going to tell him that, if I'm allowed to anyway. ... Sure, okay, I will. The guy's a real stooge. Can I say that about a senator? ... Well, he's probably going to win, so he's practically a senator. Politicians are crazy, they're all crazy. They think they can run the world and stop people from just trying to be people. Yeah, they're crazy, all of them. Next they'll be wanting us to kill a president. Good God! . . . I'm sure he was embarrassing, John, but so what? I mean, his own son is too embarrassing? He's just a kid. He doesn't even know what he's doing. . . . Yeah, okay, John, me too, gotta run. . . . I will, yeah. . . . Yep, bye."

After crossing the parking lot, he extracted his key case and opened it, but then just stood there looking at the car. He had loved the blue even in the showroom. But that was three years ago, and now it seemed to be fading. The white was still good, and the chrome. Maybe he should take Darlene down and look at the '59's. She could sit in it while he looked at that new Interceptor motor. But then he would have to listen to her all the way home, about how difficult it was going to be to pay for it, and about how inconsistent it was for a desk agent to want a new car every three years. Life was so darned stupid. She could croon away with her Elvis Presley and an hour later be crying over a Billy Graham crusade show, but he couldn't look at new cars, because he was just a desk agent and had a measly income.

Inside he pushed the wing out, shoved the footfeet all the way down once, let it up, and turned the key. From the dashboard he took the pack of Winston's and shook one out. Maybe he should change to Camel's. Turning the radio on, he dialed until he found something nice. Why should he go home for lunch anyway? Maybe he would just go to

Burger King again. She could want a color television set, but he wasn't allowed to want a new car—not a Buick or a Cadillac, which of course would be out of his range—but a Ford, just a Ford. Oh, but of course, she could want a color television to watch Perry Como. What in God's name did she see in that guy?

From the moment he pulled into the driveway he knew something was wrong. His stomach did strange things when things weren't right—never had it failed to alert him. After shutting off in the carport, he got out and opened the door to the kitchen.

The air was thick with cigarette smoke as he stepped into the kitchen. The radio was playing on the counter. Two cigarettes, still burning, were nestled on the ashtray, one with a dark lipstick mark. Hearing the front door close, he went into the hallway and saw the back of a man walking away from the house. When he got to the bedroom he stood in the doorway and looked at her as she got up, her hair mussed, and pulled on her new blouse.

"Who was that?" he queried, his stomach churning.

She would not look at him as she slipped into her shoes, but answered simply, defiantly, "Someone."

And now he could smell it in the air, even above the cigarette smoke—the pungent mix of her hot body and her perfume. "So," he said, "you were with a man?"

Still she would not look at him. Casually she got up, went to the dresser, then sat and looked at herself in the mirror. Reaching for the lipstick, she pulled off the top and gave the tube a little twist. Deftly she freshened the red lips, then looked again. Satisfied, she smacked her lips, then reached for the brush to tidy her hair.

"You have someone else?" he said. And now he saw her eyes in the mirror as they found him.

"Yes," she answered. "Yes, I have someone else—a lot of someone elses, Bud."

Turning from her, he walked back down the hallway, through the kitchen, out through the carport, and into the back yard. For a moment he stood and looked around at the leaves that had fallen during the night. Then he took up the rake and began to rake them up. He knew that he was raking the leaves, for he saw them being piled up at the end of the rake. It was funny, he considered, how nature had made both the leaves and himself and had given them purpose and beauty, only to bring them into ruin after such a short season of life.

CHAPTER 6

In his office at the police station in downtown Jacksonville detective James Tipper reached for the ashtray, then stubbed out his cigarette. Picking up the phone, he called the sergeant at the front desk. "Sergeant, it's Tipper. . . . Yeah, hi. How's it going out there? . . . Seen anything of the two I'm expecting? . . . Uh-huh, . . . Uh-huh, sure. . . . I just don't want them to wait. . . . Right, okay. . . . Sure, come and get me if you have to. . . . Okay. . . . Yep."

He hung up, then opened the door, turned on the fan, and lit another cigarette. At his desk he opened the folder and again let his eyes go over the photos of the corpse. When the phone rang, he picked up, listened for a few seconds, then hung up. Quickly he crushed out the cigarette, turned off the fan, and left.

At the front desk the sergeant pointed him toward the corner.

"Hi there," he said jovially, blinking as he approached, "I'm Detective Tipper, James Tipper. Mr. Byrne, Miss Bernard?"

In his office he shut the door, had them sit, and took a seat behind the desk. "Now," he said, smiling broadly, "I'm so glad to meet both of you. And I just want to let you know, right from the outset, this is a friendly interview, or whatever you call it—ha. Really, we're so happy you're both okay. That was a terrible incident, totally inexcusable in our society. And you don't have to say a thing, we know you were both just defending your lives. We're happy you're safe, and I'm glad to meet you."

Neither replied to this introduction, but merely sat, as if waiting for him to continue.

"All right. Now, I'm not going to bore you with a bunch of silly talk," he said, his eyes moving over Shelly's flamboyant hair and Margot's bulging muscles. "You're an artist, right? And you're a writer. Excellent. I hope you both contribute something valuable to society. Great. ... And you're both obviously very intelligent. So, no, I won't bore you with nonsense. Let me tell you straight out that this man was clearly out to kill both of you."

Margot cleared her throat, partly because of the residual smoke in the air, but also in order to speak. "Why?" she queried.

He reached for a pen, picked it up, then tossed it onto the blotter. "I was hoping one or both of you could help us with that."

"Sorry," replied Shelly. "We've tried to come up with something. But—sorry—absolutely nothing."

He picked up the pen and held it with both hands. "Well, *we* have no idea, that's for sure, not at this point anyway. So, as I said, I'm not going to bore you with nonsense. Here's what we know. Oh, and you can take this as kind of official, mainly from me, since I've done the research, but also from this department. His name was Terrence James Dahlmer. He'd been in prison for two years, but was released a short time ago."

Margot shifted on the chair. "So, you've traced him."

He tossed the pen to the blotter again, his eyes moving from Shelly's long hair to Margot's muscles, as if uncertain as to which bothered him more. "Uh—sort of. All the paperwork of his release has been lost." Here he gave each of them a short stare. And shaking his head, "You don't need to ask me, because that is all I've been able to find out, and I think I can say professionally, all anybody else is going to be able to find out. You can get yourselves a private man, but that's all he's going to be able to find out. You can trust me on this, I swear. As a detective with this department I can tell you that I have experienced this kind of thing before—not often, but at least twice before. When the paperwork disappears it disappears for a reason. And it's gone forever."

Shelly pushed his hair from his eyes. "I've got a bad feeling about this," he said.

With a grim smile, but with his eyes running curiously over the long blond hair and taking in the eyes and fair skin, "You should have a bad feeling, uh, sir. I do, too. It looks to us that someone very powerful got this man out of prison, then sent him to kill both of you. And going by Mr. Dahlmer's past record, by all accounts he should have succeeded. Miss Bernard, that was an amazing move on your part to get him between the two of you. And you both worked together with truly amazing coolness of mind and prowess. I actually have gone over it many times, and I am—well, I'm impressed. Both of you could work for us, I think. You make quite a team."

Margot looked at him, but did not reply. Since coming in she had found it difficult to breathe. The ashtray was nearly full of butts. Even from her seat she could smell the stench of his cologne, and more than once she had caught herself staring at the sharp part in his oiled hair.

"Ha, ha!" he continued. "I apologize for laughing, but we're all having a pretty good time telling your story. You threw the brick, Mr. Byrne. Maybe you should pitch for the Yankees, that was a good shot. And Miss Bernard, I'm sorry, but you've got a harder swing than Mickey Mantle. The motorcycle boys were thoroughly entertained. And my partner suggested we send a few of the criminals we bring in here around to your house and save the state some money."

"But this man," queried Shelly, "was really bad?"

"Oh yeah, he was bad. He had killed people, plural, you know. He was what we as police actually label as a killer. This is serious. That's why I'm not doing the sweet talk. You both need to walk out of here today with the knowledge that this man was intentionally extracted from prison and hired to kill you."

Shelly, his frustration building, put both hands on his head and looked at him. "Mafia?"

Tipper shook his head. "Uh—no, we don't think so. Neither of you seems to have the background of someone who even gets close to the mob. If I'm wrong, you should speak up now. Have either of you ever come in contact with anybody from the mob?"

"I know," said Margot, "that I can answer a definite no to that one."

He smiled, his eyes going again to the glamorous hair. "Mr. Byrne?"

Shelly shook his head. "Absolutely not."

"Well," he said, taking up the pen, then tossing it down, "there you go."

Margot cleared her throat again. "You said powerful people got him out of prison. How do you know they're powerful?"

He sighed, almost with a groan. "Ma'am, my brother has a full-time job and lots of hobbies. When he gets tired of one job, he gets another. I've had one job—this one—and no hobbies. When I go home at night, I think about my job. My job is all I do, all I think about, and I'm pretty good at it. Now, I don't know who these people are. If I did, I'd sure as goddamn hell go out—oh, uh, sorry for the French. But we'd go out and get them, ma'am. Only powerful people, ma'am, can do this kind of thing. We've seen it before. And that's all I can say. And we know the system out there, ma'am, and when people in the system are telling us that we're not going to get any more information."

There was a silence. Then Shelly said, "Okay. That means, then, that the people who hired him are just going to send someone else."

He nodded. "Yes, probably. I mean, maybe they'll give up, but probably they won't. They've lost very little, you see. This man was dirt, everyone's glad he's gone. But clearly he did not get himself out of prison or hire himself. You both have every right to be concerned for your lives. You also—and this is why I specifically wanted to talk to you today—you have every right to defend yourselves."

Margot's eyebrows went up. "Could you be more specific?"

Now he was particularly direct. Leaning forward, he said sternly, "Both of you—buy a gun, practice with it, and carry it everywhere."

Margot smiled. "What about a license?"

He reached behind him, retrieved a folder, and opened it. "This is where law enforcement can spit back, right into the face of crime. I don't like someone telling me the paperwork's been lost, after a guy comes to my city to murder people. That makes me so goddamn—hey, sorry again for the French. But that makes me so very, very mad! Anyway, here are your licenses, initiated by me and duly authorized by Licenses and Permits. You both may now buy and carry any weapon you want, and as much ammunition as you want, in the state of Florida. If these assholes want to lose their paperwork, I'll answer it by signing mine."

Shelly let his eyes go closed. "That's not who I am," he said. "I'm an artist, not a gunslinger."

Smiling benevolently, Tipper leaned back in his chair, then said, "Well, look at it this way. By all rights, you should be a dead artist, because this Dahlmer character was more than capable of killing you both and then just hopping off to a diner for lunch. I'm saying, you have to change your approach to life, ma'am—I mean, sir. If this had happened to my daughter, I wouldn't care if she was a nun, I'd buy her a gun and take her to the gun range every day."

Dropping his gaze, Shelly queried, "Any advice on what kind of gun to buy?"

With a sigh, as if preparing to pontificate, "Sure. Actually, the gun he used was about the best I'd recommend for you—a six-shot .38 Special. I carry one, my partner carries one, most detectives carry one. The FBI boys carry them. They're very serviceable, and they always work. You can get them anywhere."

Shelly frowned. Then, as if to show his anxiety, he stuffed some hair behind an ear, and said, "But the policeman that night called it a little popgun."

After making a clicking sound with his tongue and chuckling, "Yeah, well, that's part of their swagger, sir. The motorcycle boys are pretty much all like that. Most of them carry a .357 magnum, which will run a man down like a Harley-Davidson motorcycle. But you can trust me, sir, I carry a .38, and I don't carry a popgun. It's a lethal weapon. The recoil's minimal, so you're right on target with the next shot. With a magnum, the muzzle lift's about eight inches with every shot. And it's a bang, let me tell you. You don't need that. You need something you can feel comfortable practicing with a lot. The .38's just what you want. Please trust me on this, sir."

"And how will I know when to use it? I'm not a detective, Mr. Tipper, and I don't want to be one, or a policeman. I'm not military at all. I'm not security oriented in the least. I paint. And next time, whoever comes for us is probably not going to just call up and say he wants to come to the house to buy paintings."

When Tipper ran a hand over the top of the oily hair, as if to feel whether anything was out of place, Margot let her eyes go closed, then shot Shelly a glance. But then both listened attentively as he spoke.

"No, you're right, it probably won't be as obvious as it was this time. Again, my advice— don't be trigger happy, but if somebody approaches you in a suspicious way, well, like I'd tell my daughter, wait for him to get close, and then you pull that gun out and you pull that trigger till the goddamn thing's empty. And then, like you had only one second to live, you dump the shells and reload." Here he grabbed the pen, then tossed it again, as if satisfied, at least for the moment, that he had gotten something off his chest.

Shelly looked at him. He seemed to be such a sincere, honest man. "Sir, do you have a daughter?"

Momentarily, his eyes on the long hair, "I do, yes. She's nineteen. She's in college. She's, uh—I don't know how to say it—she's kind of mixed up. She's very beautiful, sweet, talented, and, well, a bit mixed up. I wish I had answers for her, but I don't. My wife and I love her very, very much." He stopped, as if suddenly aware that he should not have been going on. "But arm yourselves. And practice, okay?"

Shelly brought a finger to his chin. "What if we hire someone to protect us?"

"Sure. You can do that. Feel free. But those guys don't come cheap. Besides, they're visible as all hell. And you'd have to hire two of them, because there are two of you. And bodyguards have to sleep. And if someone comes for you, he'll see your bodyguard and either wait for your money to run out or just kill him and then get on with the business of killing you. You have to think this through, both of you. Whatever other steps you take, you're still probably going to end up with a self-defense situation."

"I'm not questioning your expertise, Mr. Tipper."

"I'm sure you're not. But I've tried to get to the heart of things here, and it seems like you're resisting me. . . . I've been shot five times. Three different occasions. Any of those shots could easily have killed me or maimed me for life. I have considerable expertise, sir, and I'm telling you both—you need to arm yourselves and be prepared to defend your lives."

Margot cleared her throat, then touched Shelly's arm and said simply, gently, "I trust him."

Tipper smiled at this. "Oh, and I've included in your papers here a ten-year pass to our open-field range. You want to get good with it. The trick is to kill the assailant but not the innocent donkey standing behind him. . . . And you'll notice I didn't say wound, I said kill."

CHAPTER 7

When they had gone, he switched on the fan, then pulled out a cigarette and lit it. Opening the door, he looked down the hall to make sure they had gone. At the next door, he tapped, then entered.

"Hey," he said, taking a seat. As there was no response, he contented himself for a few minutes with simply smoking and watching the fingers push the keys. But then he said, "Hey, stop typing, listen up."

Detective Dean Betts obeyed, then turned to him. "What?"

Tipper looked at him. They had been partners for nearly five years, yet the tension between them had not dissipated. He himself liked to take his time on cases, think things through. But Dean boy here—well, he always had to be in a hurry. Finally he said, "Guess who I just talked to?"

With obvious disinterest and increasing impatience, the other merely shrugged.

"I just talked to the couple from that house by the hospital."

"Yeah? And? Jimmy, come on, I've got some work to do."

"First tell me why you cut your hair. What's so great about a flattop?"

"All the kids are getting them."

"But you ain't a kid, Dean."

Not hiding his irritation, "I know I'm not a kid, Jimmy, you don't have to tell me." And with a quick shrug, "I was showing my age. Marcia said I was."

"Do you think I'd get a new haircut just because Kathy wanted me to look younger? Come on, Dean."

With an uncomfortable shrug, "I thought she was right. She's got a good head on her shoulders. She tells me what women think, how they look at men, what they want to see in them. Anyway, it's the style now."

"How do you get it to be stiff like that? What do you use on it?"

"Just hair wax. It's pretty neat. Marcia likes it, says it smells good." And lighting a cigarette, "So, what'd they say?"

"Well," and lowering his voice, as if to add intrigue, "they're a couple of oddballs, I think."

"Yeah? So, what'd you say to them?"

"Nothing. I just looked at them, talked to them. Actually, looking back on it, I gave them the best advice—you know, buy a gun, protect yourselves. I told them straight out that we had run into a wall. They're smart, they're really smart. The one that killed the guy went to that Wellesley College—

that's elite. But you should've seen her muscles. I mean, the girl was like a man, seriously. I'll bet you anything she lifts weights. Nobody can get biceps like that without lifting weights. And I'll bet, high-protein raw-egg drinks and all that. I've actually done it myself and know what I'm talking about. You should have seen her forearms. Oh, she was pretty, don't get me wrong—really pretty. But yeah, strong."

"She does body building?"

"No, no, I don't mean that. That gets grotesque—I don't mean that. But strength, you know, sort of massive strength without too much muscle mass."

"Like you get with calisthenics? I've done some of that."

"Right. But maybe with a little more mass, so she must be lifting a little bit. But impressive, I can tell you, seriously impressive. She's a hitter on a softball team. Honestly I'll bet she just taps it out of the park even on a bad day. Muscles like rocks, I'm telling you, like what men get. And that's not all. The other one, the artist, he was odd, too. He had long hair like a girl. And not just long, but beautiful, like he goes to a beauty parlor—long, blond hair, past his shoulders. His eyes were light green and kind of sparkled."

"Like a girl."

"Exactly."

Betts took a drag on the cigarette. "Probably just a fag."

"I don't know, Dean. Something stranger than that."

"Hey, Jimmy, you don't have to tell me. We've all been around. I know what's out there. Good Lord, the weirdos we pick up at that park!"

"Right, but that's what I'm saying—this guy wasn't like them."

"They're all like them, Jimmy." And taking another drag on the cigarette, "So, you helped them?"

With a nod, "I did."

"Why?"

"You really want to know why, Dean? Because I don't like some goddamn warden refusing to help me, playing ignorant on me, telling me the paperwork's been lost, and sending me away like I was some kind of dipshit. The paperwork was lost— sure, right, I'll bet. So, I not only helped them, I opened up and told them just about everything. I know an assassination attempt when I see one."

With a sniff, and talking with the cigarette between his lips, "What'd they say to that?"

"They just sat there, the man looking kind of like a woman, and the woman looking like a man, big as you please. They listened and asked intelligent questions, and I thought they were very nice."

"Was this guy at all dressed like a woman?"

"Nope. It was just the hair, the eyes, the skin. He was just too pretty to be a man. But he seemed decent enough."

"Hey, don't be saying things like that. A fag's a fag, Jimmy."

"What can I say, Dean? They both seemed like decent people."

"They're married?" And when the other shook his head, "Then, right there, they're not decent. So, don't say they're decent. They're shackin' up, Jimmy, and that's indecent."

Tipper looked at him for a moment. "We have to try and understand people. We can't just shove them around and tell them how to live. I wouldn't want to be treated like that."

Chuckling, "You ain't a fag, Jimmy."

"Well, they seemed harmless, and I helped them as much as I could. I even authorized a free range pass."

Blowing smoke out over the desk, "Okay. And?"

"And what? That's all. Isn't that enough?"

"That's the whole story?"

"Yeah, that's the whole story. . . . And I think they're going to take my advice, how about that?"

"Okay, Jimmy. Okay, fine, great."

"Damn! Nothing impresses you, Dean, you know that? You're spending too much time on your paperwork, pal." And getting up and going to the door, "Well, I'll just leave you to it. I'm goin' somewhere else. The rest of the boys are going to enjoy this. Go ahead and do your paperwork, Dean. And you'll ruin your goddamn eyes, too. I'll bet you're wearing glasses within a year."

Shelly dropped his keys onto the kitchen table and sat down. "Why would anyone do this to me?" he muttered. "I'm just a painter. I've never hurt anybody, never, not one time in my whole life. Why would anyone try to hurt me?"

After turning the faucet off, then setting the kettle on the stove, Margot replied, "Hurt?"

"All right. You want me to say it—kill."

"And by the way—*you*? Try, both of us. He asked for us both by name, Shelly."

Sighing, "He spent a long time with us today, didn't he?"

"He did."

"And you were right there with him about arming ourselves."

"Of course. The moment he said this man had been hired by somebody powerful, actually gotten out of prison and sent to kill us—God! Seriously, Shelly, yes. I can do arithmetic. I was sitting there listening to him—a couple of sentences is all it took. My mind was made up even before he suggested it—we need to arm, and do it right now, period, exclamation point."

He dropped his face into his hands, as if to hide. "I'll have a cup of tea when that boils. Could you make it?"

"English breakfast okay?"

"Sure." Then he sat down, folded his arms, and lowered his head. He let his mind go over some of the wonderful things he had always been free to think about, to want, to enjoy—art, love, friendship, free expression. Now all he wanted was peace, safety, security, tranquility. God had not made him for war, but for peace, he was sure. And yet, now this. But why?

Margot poured the tea, set the cups on the table, then sat down and looked across at the despondent eyes. Lifting her cup, she blew across it, then set it down again.

"Who have I offended?" murmured Shelly, looking up at her.

"That's not the issue. The fact that we have no idea even who it could be makes the question irrelevant. An attempt has been made on our lives in such a way that we can expect another attempt—that's the issue."

"I just want to live in peace and be able to paint. That's all. And now I've got this, and my stomach—I'm sorry, my whole goddamn mind—is so upset, I can't even enjoy a cup of tea."

"Okay. That's a description of an observation. It's accurate. And I could say the same for myself. That's great, that's just so fucking great, Shelly. But it's not the issue. The issue, as he pointed out today, is that we have to buy guns and get good with them. It's that simple. Somebody's putting money into this, so they're going to send another guy to try it again. And I'm not ruining another fucking bat."

"Hey, don't underestimate the power of wood over metal. You crushed that man's head. A gun couldn't even do that. You give me the creeps, sweetheart. With your muscles and that bat—Jesus! I know I wouldn't come after you with a gun, that's for sure."

"We were lucky, and you know it."

He took up the cup and went to the window. "Let's take the 98 and go. I think we should just move somewhere else. I think we should get ourselves lost."

She was adamant. "No. Stand and fight, it's the only way. Besides, we just renewed the lease. And I like it here. I can write."

"Yeah, okay. This could be like the Alamo, where everybody dies."

"Or how about—where everybody has a chance of living? Which is not true of the alternative. They're determined, Shelly. Running will do no good."

CHAPTER 8

The art studio, located on the second floor at the rear corner of the house, even toward the end of October, afforded enough sunlight for working from late morning until late afternoon with no more help than two electric overheads. As there were no curtains, shades were pulled down for working during the evenings. The plaster on the walls showed cracks everywhere, and in one place, where the ceiling leaked around an old chimney, flakes of the drying gypsum seemed perpetually to fall. The green linoleum, covering nearly the entire floor, was by now bespattered with paint and gesso, especially just below the three easels and two worktables.

From the beginning, Margot had considered the room to be ugly, insisting that the room at the opposite corner of the second floor should be hers for a writing studio. But Shelly, having fallen in love with the cracked walls and dingy linoleum, had considered the room to be beautiful nearly at a mystical level, insisting that even if the space was ugly, it was so only in a beautiful way. It was a place, he said, where indeed he could smear and throw paint without hindrance, where he could be as much alone as necessary to execute a work from its inception to its completion.

But yes, for Margot, who needed always to work as if flexing her muscles on a public stage, the second-floor front room was perfect as a writing studio. In summer the room was hot, but also filled with the fragrance of orange blossoms that grew in the yard. In the autumn she found herself working with the windows up to allow the breezes from the St. Johns River, a mere half block away, at the end of King Street, to blow through.

"How can you work with your door open?" Shelly asked, taking a break from his painting and leaning against the doorframe of Margot's writing studio.

"I could ask you why you prefer to work with your door closed. But I won't." And swiveling on her chair, "Because it doesn't matter, does it? What's the matter, can't paint?"

"Just taking a break."

"Want pizza tonight?"

He looked at the ceiling. "Sure."

"Great. Have it delivered. I don't feel like cooking."

After he left to call in the order, she swiveled back to the machine, typed the word *soul,* then a period, and sat back. She loved the things she had surrounded herself with. If she liked to think of herself as being strong and practical about people, she had also to admit that she was sentimental about physical objects. Her desk was littered with dictionaries, thesauruses, and other resource materials. It was lit with a single lamp. Her main typewriter was an old office SmithCorona, her portable, a newish Royal with a pressed cardboard cover. Her chair, which she had bought at a warehouse liquidation in New York, was an old wheeled job in full leather. Under her feet was a worn oriental rug that covered most of the floor. Along one wall was a long, sagging couch, where she could stretch out and give her back and mind a rest. And surrounding her were many salvaged bookcases, all full of her personal literature collected from her childhood to the present.

On impulse she moved the teacup beside the typewriter and took up the gun. Unlike Shelly, she had not needed advice as to which type of weapon and accessories to purchase. She had known immediately that the detective was correct in recommending the .38 Special. Fixed sights. No safety. Easy, immediate use. Simple reloading. No jamming. Pulling the latch, she swung the cylinder out, then returned it. With her finger on the trigger, she cocked and let down the hammer with her thumb in a single, fluid motion. No, she had not needed advice.

When they had poured tea after dinner, Shelly asked, "Can we just rake up some of those leaves tomorrow?"

"What about practice?"

"The sycamores are dirty trees. We have to get to it. It won't take that long, and then we can go to the range."

It had been three weeks since the incident, as they had come to refer to it. The floor where the man had fallen had been cleaned and the furniture in the room rearranged, but still it was difficult for them to think of the house as a safe place in which to live and create. For Shelly it had been especially difficult, and he found himself nearly constantly considering repairs and renovations to the property in order somehow to make it into a new place.

"Fine," she replied. "We'll do the leaves, then go to the range."

Setting his cup down, "Margie, are you sure this gun thing is a good idea? You're really good at it, but I'm not. I could actually hurt or kill you with it by mistake. Or I might hurt somebody else with it."

"I agree with the detective—we have no choice. But we do have to practice and get good at it."

"Do you think my work is becoming negative from all of this weapons thing?"

"Possibly."

Momentarily, "So, are you working on a new book?"

"I am."

With a sigh, "You know, Margie, I'm not sure I can make the creativity thing work with the security thing. You heard me tell the detective that. I was not kidding. You people can talk about the survival instinct all you like, but maybe mine isn't that strong."

"Then why did you throw the brick?"

"Sure, that's obviously a good point. And I'm not sure why I threw it. Maybe I was trying to save you."

"But we won."

"Maybe it was a Pyrrhic victory. My creative side just isn't, I don't know, the same as it was. I can't concentrate. I can't paint—at least, not the way I was able to before. Sometimes while I'm sitting there at my easel I look down at the gun you got me. And then I just can't go on with the painting until I get up and walk around or go to the bathroom. The gun breaks my concentration, I can't help it. I don't have a stand-and-fight mentality, which is why my solution was simply to move away."

"Even if you could get away, your safety would cost you your courage. Talk about a Pyrrhic victory, Shelly. Really? You can't see that?"

"But that's just it, I don't want to think about it. I don't want to sit and consider confronting someone with a gun or even just the workings of the gun or practicing with it or my responsibilities when carrying it in public. I don't want to think about any of it. I just want to get the problem solved so I can get on with my art."

"And you can do that—your art—without courage?"

"Oh, come on, you're being silly."

Her brow darkening, "No, I'm not. I'm asking you a very serious question. Please answer it."

"All right, I can't do my art without courage."

"I would say that courage is indispensable to art. Do you think you can run away from this threat and then expect to face your devils, as you say, in your art?"

"Maybe not, Margie, which is why I bought the gun. But the mindset itself is damaging me somehow, or at least distracting me, I know that too."

"Sorry. I'm sorry for all of it—I'm just so fucking sorry, I wish I could change it. But I can't. And you can't, either. And sure, it's affecting my work, too. But we have no choice. Nobody's suggesting we go out and find these people, just that we be prepared to defend ourselves. Other people, reasonable people, have to do this every day. There's only so much the law can do."

"And God, Margie? What about God?"

Incredulous, she pushed her bangs away. "What about him? Oh, and you're not religious, so why the hell are you bringing religion into it?"

"Can't God protect us?"

"You're not thinking, are you? Maybe God has already given us the ability to protect ourselves. I have nothing against trusting God. If you want to trust God, trust that he made that detective do all that paperwork, shove licenses into our hands, and then advise us to go and buy guns. Do you know how hard it is to get a license to carry a gun? Talk about a miracle. Jesus!"

CHAPTER 9

"Hey," said the sergeant, "you ladies shoot pretty good!"

Shelly merely cleared his throat and looked down at this, while Margot set their tackle box of shooting equipment on the plywood table.

"And you," he went on, pointing an impudent finger at Margot, "you're a hotshot, you are. Did you ever shoot with the police?"

She gave him a look, then replied, "Let's just say I knew one."

"Uh-oh," he returned, pulling his chin in and sticking his chest out, as if to emphasize the starched pleats in his military-like shirt, "that doesn't sound good. At least you weren't dumb enough to marry one."

"Actually I was," she said dryly. "But it didn't last long."

"Yeah? Okay. Was he the one that showed you how to shoot?"

"Not really. But he did show me what assholes men can be."

He let his eyes run over her muscular arms. "Oh, there's some pretty nasty women out there, too, ma'am, I think I can vouch for that. . . . But you know, lady, you can shoot. I saw the way you dumped and reloaded there. You ain't a part-timer. You're a hotshot. Here, let me see those targets. . . . Yeah, well, see, that's what I'm sayin'. Okay, here's one at thirty feet—look at this group, five inches max, and you weren't shootin' slow. Let me see the sixty-foot one. Oh my God! Ma'am, police can't even shoot like this. Sixty feet, double action, shootin' pretty fast, you put eighteen shots in about a nine-inch group. Damn! Congratulations, you've got my admiration, lady."

On the drive home Shelly said, "Maybe I should just cut my hair."

"Why?"

"Maybe I look a little too feminine for these people. Everywhere we go people seem to take me for a girl."

"Jesus, Shelly! You are half a girl, so who cares? They stare at my muscles more than your hair. We should have a contest—I'll bet I'd win." And after pulling into a parking lot, she switched off and sat looking at him. "Besides," she said, "you're just my style. Maybe I'll buy you some panties."

"This is a gun shop, isn't it?"

"It is. Come on."

The proprietor seemed unhappy that he must deal with women. "What can I help you ladies with?" he drawled.

When Shelly replied that he wasn't sure, Margot pulled her sunglasses off and replied, "Me and my boyfriend here want to get a shotgun, maybe a pump 12. Say, the 870."

"Oh, sorry," he came back quickly, glancing at Shelly's hair. "I thought you was a girl. My mistake." Then, clearly unhappy, he said to Margot, "Well, you don't want that, ma'am. That's a police gun. Kicks a bit, might hurt your arm." But then, his eyes going to her rocky shoulders, "Or maybe not." And reaching behind him, he drew the shotgun from the shelf. He opened it, handed it to her, and said, "I can get you the .410, though, if you want."

"No thanks," she returned, taking the gun from him. "A .410's for birds and snakes. I never kill either one." And closing the gun, she sighted it along the countertop to the clock on the wall. Not looking at him, she said, "I'll take it." And handing it back to him, "And give me three boxes of double aught and two of slugs.

"Okay," he said, "you got it! Let me grab the ammo. Remington 870 12 gauge—I'll ring it right up, lady."

That evening after dinner, they took out the .38's and practiced around the house, darting around corners, rolling on the floor, with the lights on and then off. Loading, ejecting, drawing from the small-of-the-back leather holsters, and from a purse. After Margot, flipped the gun from behind her back to catch it in front with the same hand, Shelly simply blew his breath in amazement.

"You've done this a lot, haven't you? So—your husband?"

"My asshole cop ex-husband," she corrected.

"You never refer to him by name. Sometimes you just say Joey, but that's all."

"Joseph Lucci. Yeah—Joey."

Momentarily, "Do you ever miss him? I mean, you know—"

"His dick? Nope. Or anything else about the goddamn fool."

"Did you like it that he was a cop?"

"Well, actually, before I knew him, he was just a thug. He had worked as a thug, too, for some people. He was never specific about who they were, so I just let it go. But then he became a cop, I met him, and married him. Yeah, we used to play guns in the house."

"Like we just did."

"Not quite, Shelly, that was practice. But Joey liked to actually play, like a teenager. He even shot at me once, a magnum, then just fell down laughing. God! I thought I'd lost my hearing. . . . But then I left him and applied to Wellesley."

"Looking for love?"

"Maybe just a multifaceted person. Joey was a simple guy."

"Well, I love it that you can write novels, shoot guns, lift weights, and fix cars."

"And kill people?"

Dubiously, "Maybe not so much that."

"So, you like my masculine side?"

He looked at her for a moment. "I can still see you sitting there as I walked in that day. Jeez, those muscles!"

"Gave you a hard-on, huh?"

"Practically."

She looked at her watch. "This is silly talk. Practice is over. I'm going to take a shower. It's been a long day for me."

December

Winter could be an awkward season for Jacksonville. Some of its inhabitants, used to the visual scheme of Spanish moss, palm trees, and old Southern architecture, found the experience of freezing temperatures truly disconcerting, even threatening. But for those who had come from harsher climates, the experience of having a shorter, milder winter with a longer, more tropical summer was positively lovely. For Shelly and Margot the climate was the perfect mixture.

"God!" uttered Shelly on a morning early in January. "It started, but it seemed like it wasn't going to. Maybe we should call them."

She stopped typing. "It's not a new car."

"But they said it was *like new*. Am I not to take that literally?"

She gave him a twisted smile. "Not unless you lower your IQ."

"They are never helpful when I call them. And when I took it in that time, the service manager spent the whole time staring at my hair and my ass."

"Tie your hair up."

"They were supposed to be a pretty good dealer."

"If you want me to take it in, Shelly, I will. Did you push the accelerator down once and let it up before turning the key, like I said?"

Glaring at her, "Yes, I pushed it down, Margie, all the way down—once—let it up—and then turned the fucking key, all right? And it started, but like some old man getting out of bed in the morning. Isn't there something you can check?"

"Did my alimony come?"

"It did. We're rich. But I don't want to spend it on our *like-new* car, okay? Or on more guns."

Turning back to the typewriter, "I don't actually need to look at it. It sounds like the battery. I'll pick one up at Western Auto and put it in myself. It's pretty simple."

"Then why didn't you say so, Margie?"

"Or we could just wait for warmer weather, and the battery wouldn't have that much of a problem."

"So," said Tipper, reaching for his cup, "I was thinking we could look at getting a new car."

"Could or should?"

"Take your pick. You're the pretty girl that's going to have to drive it most of the time."

"Don't you flatter me, James Tipper. It's only five years old, and it only has forty thousand miles on it."

"Forty-eight."

She looked over at him. He was not, she knew, a man given to wanting things. He was not at all like that, like her father had been, or like Dean, who seemed to need some new costly thing or even a pair of shoes every week or month. Marcie, she knew from shopping with her, bought a new dress practically every week. And of course, it didn't stop there, for it wasn't just things they wanted, but new styles, like Marcie getting Dean to have that new flattop haircut. Why, for goodness' sake would she do that? But no, thank God, her Jimmy wasn't like that. He seemed to mean business in everything he did. Which of course made him perfect for the career he was in. So, if he suggested they buy something, even something big, like a car, she must take him seriously.

"I suppose," she replied, "we could look. I'm glad we got the Biscayne, I like it. Could we just get a new one? Maybe one in a different color or with a different interior, that would be wonderful. But the Impala's a little too fancy for us. We don't need fanciness, Jimmy."

"The Elders have an Impala, and she's just a school teacher. Where does she teach?"

"Anne? West Riverside. It's a pretty car, I admit, and Anne's certainly the ticket."

"Ticket?"

"Well, I think she's quite attractive."

Rolling his eyes, "She's pretty, yes, very pretty, but not terribly glamorous. I mean, be honest—it's the car, the big sporty, silver Impala. Wouldn't you like one of those to wheel around town in?"

She looked away. "It would be nice. What year is it?"

"It's a '58, with skirts and the Continental kit."

"I don't know what all that is, but it's certainly sleek. Do you think we could afford one?"

"It is sleek, but it's not a Cadillac, so I think we'll be all right. We'll look at the '59's. They've got fins. I don't know if the Continental kit's available, and you wouldn't like the sporty look anyway."

She stared at him. "Why wouldn't I like the sporty look? What are you saying?"

With a shrug, "Come on, Kathy, you know you'd feel self-conscious after a couple days driving it."

"Well—let's go and take a look at one."

"Makes sense. Yeah, we'll go look. Think of a color."

"Not silver like Anne's," she returned. "Maybe red or white."

"You know her by her first name?"

"I do, Jimmy. She's very nice. She teaches sixth grade there."

He cleared his throat. "So, did he say anything when you told him?"

"Father Galligan?"

"Himself."

"You're English, Jimmy, don't start with the accent."

"Aye, but me better half, a-sittin' with me here at the table, is Irish to her Cork core."

"How do you actually know I'm from Cork, Jimmy?"

"You told me."

"And why should you be believin' me? The Irish always lie to the English, otherwise they'd be shot."

He loved this lady, and he loved her when she was this way—full of sparkling, dark humor, keen intelligence, and skillfully aimed wit. He loved her green eyes, her body. How could he not love a woman who could be mean as hell while cooking him a lovely dinner? How could he not love a woman who both loved the Church and had an ass right out of heaven?

After taking a sip of his tea, "So, what did he say?"

"He said he was sure we could handle it. He said all young girls today are mixed up."

He looked at her, then, with disappointment, replied, "Okay."

She set her cup down hard. "What did you want him to do, Jimmy, counsel her? If you don't know your own daughter, I can tell you myself, she wouldn't even show up. Father Galligan knows her, too, which is why he didn't offer to counsel her."

"Kathy, I'm the one who should have known better than to have you ask a priest. And Galligan—really? The man's a goddamn IRA priest!"

"Yeah, and you can say a good count of Hail Marys for that remark. You're a bit of a profane man, James Tipper. Besides, I like him."

"I'll bet you do, sure. County Cork, and all that, sure."

"You know, you should have married a Loyalist. But you didn't."

"I know I didn't. You wouldn't even be loyal to the Catholic Church, if it ever seriously crossed you."

"It hasn't crossed me yet."

"Maybe not. But it hasn't given us a sensitive priest. He's a hard-noser, he's meaner than you are, and I should have known better than to have you ask him anything about it."

With a sigh, "Jimmy, in the end, Molly's our daughter. We're responsible. No matter what kind of advice we get from the Church or anyone else, we have to deal with it. And I'm sorry, Jimmy, but she's not a bad girl. She's just confused."

"Or maybe not."

"Okay," she returned, reaching for her tea, "or maybe not. But people are starting to say now, you know, that they have a right to be who and what they want to be. And I think there's something to it. People have a right to be who they are."

"That's fine, Kathy. You believe that, and I believe that. But right now society, which means the Church and the law, well, they don't see it that way."

"I'm not saying I agree with the Church or the law on everything. I'm a faithful Christian and a good citizen, but I will decide for myself what I consider to be right or wrong."

"That's fine. We've been over this before. We've talked it to death. And yeah, we'll talk about it some more. But our daughter is coming into conflict with this college. And my guess is, they're not about to change their rules for her. She may leave, she may just walk out, I don't know. But she's so goddamn upset, I'm seriously worried about her, I think we both are. I mean, we both talked to her on the phone—and this is one hell of a troubled soul."

CHAPTER 10

Practice with the .38's soon became a regular activity. Not comfortable with spending so much time at the police range, they found a private outdoor range and continued there at least once a week throughout the colder months. At home they finished each day with practice around the house. Every room, including bathrooms and kitchen, was tested and retested for scenarios. On weekends they would take water pistols and a kid's toy pop rifle out into the yard, the car, and the garage to simulate dealing with possible outside attacks.

The slogan for every day became *always paint, always write, always practice.* And as Margot added, eating, drinking and kissing were optional. It was she who insisted on proficiency with the .38's for both of them. As she had learned from working with her husband on his police rounds, survival meant that the first defense was usually the last defense, and if anything could go wrong, it would go wrong. Her perspective was simple, practical, and nonmoralistic. The point, she said, was never to stop an intruder, it was, as Detective Tipper had emphasized, to kill him. And when reminded that the *him* might turn out to be a *her,* she threw back that hesitating to kill a woman because she was a woman could prove fatal.

Spring 1960

In the spring four of Shelly's new abstracts were taken on consignment at a small downtown gallery, and Margot's book was accepted, following two revisions, by a publisher in Boston. As the news of both arrived within the same week, Saturday was targeted for celebration and perhaps a little debauchery.

"We will go to dinner," said Shelly.

"And a movie."

"A drive-in movie?"

"Why not? And we can throw popcorn out the windows and have sex in the back seat."

He wrinkled his nose at this. "Now, don't get ahead of the culture." Then, looking into the brown eyes, "Are we happy, Margie?"

Momentarily, "No."

"But I want to be happy. Do you think we'll ever be happy?"

"I doubt it. But if you want a palatable answer— I think we're as happy as any couple could expect to be."

But seeing the eyes begin to well up, she put her arms around him and told him not to cry. "I am sorry I can't just make you happy. I wish I had the power, but I don't. Please don't cry, Shelly, please don't. I don't know much about happiness myself, but I want to have it for both of us."

On a Saturday in May they drove to Memorial Park on Riverside Avenue, where Margot was to play with the Avondale A's and another local team in a three-inning demonstration game for the community. Shelly, with coffee and a pastry, watched from a bench as the teams took to the field and the game began.

From the end of the park, near the river, came the intrusive sounds of model airplanes being flown by a group of boys. Finishing his coffee, he stretched his arms and walked over to watch as some of the planes were being refueled.

"Is that gasoline?" he queried a boy as he squeezed fuel from a small rubber bulb.

"No, ma'am, it ain't. It's model airplane fuel."

"What kind of engine is that?"

The boy grinned up at him. "It's a McCoy 35, and it'll chop your fingers up, if you don't start it right."

"Yes, I would imagine. The other engines have sounded really loud and powerful. Where did you get this one?"

"I built the plane out of a kit I got from King Street Hobby. And I got the motor there too. Want to see me fly it?"

He watched as the boy clipped battery cables to the motor, then repeatedly gave the propeller a spin with his finger. When suddenly the engine screamed to life and profusely blew its exhaust toward him, he stepped back. Quickly the boy unclipped the cables, then stood up proudly with the plane. He grinned back admiringly, but stayed where he was. Suddenly the boy took a step toward him and simply handed him the plane.

"Let it go when I nod, okay?" the boy yelled above the scream of the motor. Then he ran, took up the handle attached to the control cables, and gave the nod.

Shelly let the roaring plane go, then backed away again as it jumped into flight. But after only four complete circles around the boy, the plane dived, hit the ground with a pop, and broke into pieces.

"Shit!" the boy yelled, slamming the handle to the ground.

It was then that Shelly saw him—a man with a camera in his hands, standing beyond the boy and near the trees. He wore dark pants, a sort of sport shirt under a gray sport jacket, and an off-white hat with a dark band. He had black-rimmed glasses on, but was close enough for Shelly to see that he was not really watching the game, but was scanning the players, as if looking for someone. Sporadically he raised the camera and snapped pictures of various players, including two or three of Margot and even eventually of himself as he still stood near the boy.

As the boy approached with pieces of the broken plane in his hands Shelly queried whether such planes crashed often.

"Yes, ma'am, and it takes a long time to build one again." And holding up the engine, "But the McCoy's okay. You can't hurt a McCoy."

Shelly smiled, wished the boy good luck, and with his eyes still on the man leisurely made his way back to the bench, where he took a few sips from the cup and pretended to be watching the game. Why now, he wondered? Why not simply allow the beautiful day, with its perfect weather, its happy voices, its innocent ball game, to continue? Why interrupt it with a sinister-looking man obviously not interested in the activities? Why did life do things like this? Because life was mischievous. It tiptoed around you until you were seduced by one of its pretty blue skies, then caught you just as you were looking up, showed you one of its awful dangers, and laughed like hell as it frightened the fucking death out of you.

Putting the cup down, he felt under his shirt for the holster riding on his belt at the middle of his back—not to make sure the gun was there, of course, but to make sure it was easily accessible.

"I'm still shaking," he said later as they sat in the restaurant. "Margie, my stomach flipped when I saw him. I knew somehow that I was the reason he was there, that we both were. He was pretty far away, but I could see he wasn't following the game at all—he was watching and taking pictures of the players, especially of you and me.

With a shrug, "I know, I saw him."

"Don't treat it like that, Margie, this is important."

She leaned closer and dropped her voice. "I know that, I'm the one pushing the gun practice."

"But you're not scared, obviously."

Margot took up her beer. "I *am* scared."

"No, you're not, and it's annoying."

"He was creepy, right? I think we've got ourselves a scout."

"He may have followed us there."

"Shelly, it was an advertised public event."

"How did he know you were on the A's?"

"I don't know. But I think our Detective Tipper gave us a lot of information for a reason. Whoever is after us isn't quitting, and they know a lot about us. In fact, they could be watching us right now."

Slowly Shelly let his eyes move over the other patrons. "Let's just go. I can't enjoy my food."

She speared a piece of fish, put it into her mouth, and began to chew contentedly. "You'll be fine. And please don't look at me like that."

"Like what?"

"Like I'm supposed to do something about all of this."

With a troubled sigh, "Why are you so calm? What makes you that way?"

"I'm not calm, I'm upset. But I have to eat and sleep and take a shit, right? I have to go to the store and the gas station and the library, right? And by God, I have to play my fucking softball games too. But I can't do anything about any of this more than I'm doing, so let's not turn on each other, because that would only help them."

Suddenly the waiter approached. "Excuse me, ladies," he said politely, "but could I ask you to keep it down a little? And please watch the language, if you don't mind. I wouldn't have said anything, but we've had a complaint."

Riverside Avenue, usually nearly mystically serene, seemed eerie as they drove in silence. Traffic was modest. Through the windshield the

Spanish moss hanging from the old trees seemed like gray-green clouds flying over them.

"Has anybody been following us?" he queried as she braked for a curve.

"Not really."

Momentarily, "You know, Margie, I have to bring something up that's been bothering me about all of this. I don't want you to get upset, but I have to get it out, okay? You said back there that you're upset, too."

"I am."

"Just listen. Actually, I would say you haven't been genuinely upset about any of it. Even when that guy was in our house you didn't seem to be that upset. I was terrified, but you weren't even frightened. I watched you hit him and then beat him to death, like in some bizarre movie. Or—like you had done it before."

She cleared her throat. "Maybe I've watched a lot of movies."

He ran a hand through his hair, pushing it from his eyes to see her better. "Yeah, and maybe you're just fucking lying to me. Don't play with me— don't fucking play with me, Margie. I don't like it, seriously. I'm very upset here. Now, I'm getting this out, and I want you to be objective and serious and not talk down to me."

"You were calm enough to throw the brick, Shelly. And you squarely hit him, too."

"I was frantic."

"You seemed pretty calm, to me."

The green eyes narrowed in the darkness. "Not like you. You were different, like you'd done it before. . . . So, tell me. Had you done it before?"

Momentarily, "Okay, I worked with my husband a little on the streets. I'd go out in the patrol car with him when his partner was sick. His partner was an alcoholic and a lot of times just couldn't get himself out of the house. Anyway, I went out with my husband—with my fucking asshole husband Joey—and yeah, saw some stuff and did some stuff. So, is that enough, or do you want to hear more? Because I'm not going to tell you much more. Jesus! I could probably go to prison over some of it, okay?"

"Did you kill anybody?"

"Yes. But only twice."

"My God! You actually killed someone—two people? God!"

"We were attacked. The police have a right to defend themselves, too, you know."

"But you were just riding along?"

"Sort of, yeah. But I was attacked, too, since I was in the car. So?"

"What did you use?"

"Once, his shotgun. Buckshot can't really be traced. Slugs can be, a little, but not buckshot, especially when used in an urban setting. And these were just street fights really. The other time, I used a .38 he had taken off somebody and just kept in the car. It was untraceable."

He pushed more of the hair back, looked over at her profile, then back through the windshield. How had he gotten into this mess? By simply loving this woman? God! Was life ugly, or what? Why was life or God or whatever doing this to him? Why? Then he heard her voice.

"You're not saying anything, Shelly. You're thinking, but you're not saying anything."

"Right. Well, what is there to say? You're very different from me. I thought we were so much alike, but we're not. We're very different."

"So? Then we fit together as complements. Opposites maybe, but still, we were attracted to each other and here we are—attacked together and surviving together. And I hope, still in love, at least I am with you."

Later, as they lay awake in bed and the silence became unbearable she said softly, "You didn't reply, Shelly."

"I know."

"Could you reply?"

"Of course I love you. . . . But I'm different from you. You can talk about being one soul all you want, but my soul isn't constructed the way yours is. It's softer, a lot softer. I don't know machines or weapons. I don't have muscles. And if you want to know the truth, I have serious doubts that I could actually kill somebody even if I was attacked."

"But you like my muscles, right?"

"Yes, I do. You've got a hard side physically that I just plain adore. I like everything about it— your muscles, your smell, your prowess, your ability with mechanical things. But you've also got a hard side philosophically, intellectually, and maybe even morally, that makes me very uncomfortable."

Momentarily, "Do you think I'm immoral?"

"Of course not. But you can kill and create within the same mindset. Most people can't do that, they can't make those things work together.

You not only can do it, you seem to be able to do it easily."

"So, taking both sides of me, all of me together as a person, do you still want to love me?"

He slipped an arm over her stomach. "Yes. . . . But I'll tell you, girl, you sure scare the shit out of me sometimes."

CHAPTER 11

After putting water on to boil, Shelly sat down at the kitchen table. Gently he began to massage his cheek, for the tingling sensation was now beginning to dissipate and was being replaced by a definite itch.

"So," said Margot, coming in with her cup, "what did he say?"

"It was just a filling. I was so relieved."

"Good news. Okay. Is there enough water in that for me?"

"Would you say Dr. Phillips is an alcoholic?"

She shrugged, then sat down. "He might be. But who cares? When we get to the next tax bracket, sweetheart, we'll go to a better dentist. But for now, he's great. And he's across the street. How about the water? Is there enough for me?"

"Oh. Uh—you know, I didn't think. They said nothing hard or hot. I'd burn my mouth anyway. So, you take it."

As the kettle began to whistle she got up turned the dial to off, then filled her cup and dropped in a teabag. Taking her seat again, she pulled the string to move the bag up and down. "Still numb?"

He shook his head. "No. It's starting to hurt."

"Are you going home again?"

"For the Fourth? I haven't heard from mom or dad in months. Maybe they don't want me this year."

"Maybe I'm the one they don't want."

"No, it's me. You just make it worse, but it's definitely me."

"They're afraid people will find out what a weird son they've got and what a weird girl he lives with. So, your dad's really going to run for the senate?"

Again he began to rub the cheek. "I'm sure he is. But if he wins and in a couple of years decides to run for president, can you imagine my mom as first lady?"

"How much is in the account?"

"The checkbook says about five hundred. When's your money coming in for the book?"

"Soon. Five thousand."

With a groan, "That's a lot of money. I can't wait to have it safely in the account."

"How about the gallery?"

He stopped rubbing the cheek. "They have one out. I'm sure the people just want to see if it goes with their curtains. But if they take it, our portion will be two hundred. I have plenty of supplies. But if I run low, I'll just work smaller."

"Which would mean doing more nudes?"

He nodded. "But, you see, I have this French girlfriend and won't have to pay her much for modeling."

The brown eyes became mischievous. "I know when I'm being talked about." And pulling off her top, "So, I'm still your model?"

His eyes moved over her skin. "Yes, you are still my model."

"Well," she returned, with a coy look, "I'm still cheap. But I have to let you know, kisses have gone up to a dollar."

In his studio, still giving his chin an occasional rub, he closed the door, then sat for a moment before the easel. Then he got up and began to pull the desk drawers open and to make a mental count of the tubes of paint and of other materials. Fourteen medium-size tubes of color, five large of flake white. And pulling out another drawer, about a quart left each of oil and turp, and a pint of Dammar. Numerous new flat bristles and flat and round sables. Three boxes of soft charcoal sticks. Five boxes of staples, and the 900 was full. Throwing a glance at the racked boxes—plenty of strips. Finally, he unhooked the strap from the partial rolls of canvas in the corner bin and looked at their ends. Good, there was plenty.

Before sitting again, he looked at himself in the long mirror. High humidity always increased the natural wave of his hair, but also so dulled it that he didn't want to look at it. Following the image down, he was glad he had a pretty body. Reddish-blond hair, green eyes, pale pearly skin.

"What's this?" said Margot, pushing the door open suddenly. "Hey, take the clothes off, if you're going to look at yourself. Planning a self-portrait?"

"I'm considering it. But maybe just from the waist up. What do you think?"

Falling into the overstuffed chair and throwing a leg over, "Well, I've seen your ass, and it's truly worthy. But since I'm the model under contract, I'm starting to feel jealous just thinking about it. You don't want to make me your competition, do you?"

He sat down at the easel. Giving the crank a turn to raise the shelf, he queried, "Did the mail come?"

"Nope."

"Want to watch the set tonight?"

"Sure. What's on?"

"I have no idea."

"It sounds adventurous, then. And how about dinner, what would you like? I'm cooking tonight."

With a shrug, "Spaghetti would be nice. And there's ground beef."

"Perfect. And I know we have the pasta. And we'll open the Cabernet to make it a French and Italian dinner. Too bad we can't get a little of your Irish in there."

"I'm half English—my mom."

"Well," she said, "now we're getting complex."

"I've never been to France. You should take me, show me around."

Flexing her arm muscles, and without looking up, "We'll go. You'll love it. I've never been to Ireland."

Watching the muscles bulge, "I'll take you. You'll love it."

With a sigh, she looked at him for a moment. "You're not happy, are you, Shelly?" And when the answer was delivered by a mere shake of the head, "Why? I mean, I know that's a simplistic, an unrealistic question, but isn't there something you can say to help me connect with your negative side? I do want to connect."

"I don't know," he returned. "Maybe it's the way I was designed."

"Okay. I empathize with that. We've all been designed. I see myself as having a choice and the power to choose. I'm not a victim of either design or influence. And I don't think finger pointing's going to be allowed in the next life."

"I'm not sure where I stand on all that. I do believe in God, in Jesus, in whatever hell else there is that's true. And I know I'm responsible for everything in my sphere, my circle, okay? But I don't know how to apply that principle. I feel lost and sad."

With a sigh, she got up and went to the doorway. "I'm sorry you're not happy. Personally I think anybody as intelligent and talented and nice looking as you are should be very happy. If I looked like you, I would be in love with myself."

He did not reply.

"Why don't you start that self-portrait," she said. "I'm going to work for another hour or so. We'll have dinner about five."

Summer

A few minutes before five, Shelly wiped the turp brush, stuck it into the oil jar, and left for the kitchen. At the landing he could smell the ground beef and spaghetti sauce cooking.

"Anything I can do?" he queried, entering the steamy kitchen.

"Open the wine and wash the studio shit off those hands. We got a letter from Sally. She and Michael have finished their courses for the year and want to come for a visit."

"That's crazy. She should take him to Europe. They're going to hate the heat down here."

Two days later, as the doorbell was being persistently rung, Shelly, his hand on the grip of the .38 under the back of his shirt, peeked through the side glass, then pulled the front door open.

"I cannot believe this," he exclaimed, giving Sally and Michael a welcoming hug. And catching the gleam of Sally's red Eldorado convertible at the curb, "And you drove? That car's going to need a wash."

"I'm just glad it got us here," replied Sally with an aristocratic air. "It's new and hasn't been properly tuned for racing. And we did race down here—couldn't wait to see you two. That's what I do every year at the end of my studies—I pick up the phone call a bunch of people all over creation and then just get in the car and drive to the end of the world. That's where we are, right? Or is it hell? It's certainly hot enough."

Later, Margot, who was frying hamburger in an open skillet, told them over her shoulder how the man had called not only for Shelly but herself, obviously intending to kill them both.

Shelly then took up the narrative and described the killing of the man and how the motorcycle cops had strode in with their guns drawn. He related how Margot and he had come to be armed, how they had been directed by the detective to buy and carry guns and be prepared to defend themselves. He described how they practiced every day around the house and often at the range. He showed them his hidden holster, then pulled the gun, swung its cylinder out, and showed them the cartridges.

"So," said Margot, putting the food on the table, "you should know that it's actually not safe here."

But when Michael said the dangers didn't bother him at all, and Sally chimed the same, they all took up their wine and vowed to face together whoever else might come for them.

"Actually," said Sally, "New York is becoming quite dangerous. This might be instructive for us, and certainly fun. I've never been shot at before."

So it was decided, since Michael, as a political science major and future picket liner, and Sally, as a journalism major and bored aristocrat, were both eager for the experience, that they should move in and stay until their return for Columbia's fall semester.

CHAPTER 12

Like Shelly, neither Michael nor Sally had had previous experience with weapons. Both were equally shocked at how loud the actual blast was from a handgun as opposed to what they were used to hearing via television and movies. At first, Sally jumped at every shot from the .38's, and nearly fell backward at the sound from a .357 magnum being fired in the next lane. Michael, however, seemed to take to the whole idea, and within the hour of range time had overcome his natural tendency to flinch when nearby weapons were discharged.

Within a week after their moving in, Sally had purchased for them a handgun, a holster, and ammunition. Although they were not licensed to publicly carry the weapon, still they wished to have their own to use at the range and to keep nearby at the house.

But after a month of exposure to Margot's instructions in firearms usage and responsibility, both Sally and Michael expressed concern for the effect such a weapons perspective seemed to be having on their general outlook on everyday life. Sally said she did not want to live in police mode, as she put it, as it seemed to restrict her naturally carefree spirit. Michael, agreeing, complained that since taking up a gun his ability to concentrate upon ideology as a sphere had been hampered.

"I could never," he said to Margot and Shelly, "carry a gun. It's hard enough on my psyche now being responsible for one here at home. But getting a license like you two have? I could never do that and still be who I am."

"You might change your mind," said Margot, "if we're attacked. If learning to use a gun changes a person's thinking, so does being attacked. This isn't the military, but none of us wants some moron to simply walk through the front door and kill us. We all want to have a fighting chance."

"But getting a license to carry a gun," argued Michael, "is weirdly different from defending yourself at home. Now you're going out into the public with something that could hurt other people, innocent people, even kids. And what would it do to a kid—maybe some little girl on her bicycle, holding her doll and eating a popsicle—to see you gun somebody down? Maybe the detective didn't think of that when he advised you to be ready to defend yourselves in public."

But Margot returned, "And what would it do to that kid to watch you gunned down without even trying to defend yourself—to watch as you simply permitted some goofy malignant entity of society to murder you? Come on, Michael, you're an idealist, I'm sure you can conjure an acceptable answer."

"Idealist? Is it idealistic to want a system where the police are trained and paid to be in police mode so that the public won't have to be? I don't want a power-based society, I want a law-based society."

"Michael, I'm not marching out into public trying to solve my problems with a gun. But I have a right to defend myself even when I go to the store."

"And I agree with that," put in Shelly. "I don't have a security or military mentality, either, Michael. But I know that in most cases the police come after the fact. They know it, too, which is why they advised us to carry weapons. And what's the alternative, to turn that little girl on her bike over to a society where the criminals are allowed to bully the people? I don't think so. Margot has helped me to see that."

"But you're an artist," he returned. "And Margot's a writer. People in the arts are supposed to be sensitive, society expects them to be, so they can paint and write about deep things, beautiful things. I mean, who in the arts had guns?"

"I was wondering the same thing, so I did a little research. Many people in the arts had guns. Some even carried them. They didn't see having a gun as incongruous with being an artist. Some of the Impressionists took a gun when they went to paint in Fountainbleau. Van Gogh had a gun."

"Yeah, and used it on himself."

"Not the point, Michael. The point is that he didn't see it as antithetical to his art. Even Jascha

Heifetz has a gun. Historically lots of artists, writers, and musicians did."

"Well, I would think the majority of them just couldn't do that."

Margot smiled. "If I don't have the courage to face my enemies, where will I get the courage to face my demons as a writer? Finding truth takes courage."

Michael gave his nose a swipe. "What about all these nuns around here? I've seen them. They're pretty hard to miss with those uniforms."

"Habits," corrected Sally.

"Okay. I don't care what you call them. St. Vincent's is obviously very Catholic, and the Catholic Church is against violence. I'll bet, if they knew you had guns here, a bunch of them would grab you and throw you into that river. They would say that guns are antithetical to their faith."

"Hey," said Margot, "if we're going to bring religion into it, let's get things straight. Faith is faith, and religion is religion. Faith is believing, religion is doing, it's pretty simple."

With a chuckle, "Yeah, well who the fuck cares about that? For most people the terms are interchangeable, like force and violence."

"They're different, too. Force is force, that's all, but violence is force that violates. If all force was violence, no one, including the police, could ever legally use force. You know, you'd better get your definitions straight, if you're headed for the picket lines. Sally, you're the journalist, you should buy him a dictionary."

"I'm not a journalist yet," she replied. "And if I become one, I'm not writing articles about either politics or religion, thank you very much."

"Yeah," said Shelly, "good luck with that. You'll have to ignore just about the whole world."

"Like you said, faith and religion are different. If I want to have faith, I want to have it on my terms, not somebody else's. And do I need organized religion? No thank you."

Michael looked at her. "No synagogue for you, huh?"

"Sure, I'll take synagogue, Michael, if I want to," she shot back. "But I don't want to. Maybe I don't want to right now, but I don't want to. Maybe tomorrow I will, who knows? But I want the choice to be mine."

Then he asked Margot and Shelly, "How about these nuns around here, have they come after you with their crosses yet?"

"Nope," returned Margot. "But if they do, I think I'll invite them in and give them some tea."

Grinning, "Yeah, then you'll turn Catholic."

"Probably not, Michael. But I probably would sooner than I'd become an anarchist."

"Like me?"

With a shrug, "You sure seem to fit the description."

"So did you when you were at Wellesley. You were quite the rebel, you said yourself."

"And I still am, when the system steps out of line."

"It seems to step out of line a lot, doesn't it?"

"It does," she returned, pushing the bangs from her eyes. "But I'm not going to burn my own house down just because it needs some repair work. I'm fine with the system, and I'm fine with religion too."

"You're quite the preacher. Which is odd, since you're not religious at all in your writing."

"I may be ungodly, Michael," she returned, "but I'm not godless."

Shelly cleared his throat gently. "I'm a fairly cynical person," he said. "But I believe in God, and I believe in having some kind of religion, even joining an organized group of some kind, a church. I don't belong to a church, but I wouldn't mind it."

Sally stared at him. "I hate to tell you, but you swear too goddamn much to ever join a church. If these nuns heard you talk, they wouldn't just throw you in the river, they'd take you to the sink and wash your mouth out with soap."

"I still don't understand," said Michael, turning to Margot, "I mean, putting the gun thing aside, how you can write, with blood on your hands."

"Well," she returned, "that's what I'm saying. I don't have blood on my hands, Michael. That bastard would have had it on his hands, if I hadn't stopped him."

"You make too many distinctions. I'm not sure everybody makes the distinctions you do."

"I'm sure they don't. Too bad."

Now he laughed out loud. "So, you swear like a sailor and believe in God. You've killed a man, but don't have blood on your hands. And you carry a gun, but you're not violent. . . . You're weird, that's what you are."

"So," said Sally, as if tired of listening to the exchange, "there was actually blood all over this floor? How did you get it cleaned up? Did you call somebody?"

Margot looked at her, then answered, with a quick shrug, "No, I just cleaned it up with a little bleach, then threw the mop out."

In August, Sally and Michael packed the Eldorado and headed back to New York. Clearly they were looking forward to their return to school. Besides, confessed Sally, she was tired of having sex in a sweat. She suggested that Florida should seriously consider changing its nickname to The Sauna State.

The combination of rain and sunny humidity brought such sultry weather to the rest of the summer that Shelly found himself simply unable to paint. The sweaty air, as he called it, had permeated even his creativity. When he went around the house shirtless, Margot called him a shameless naked girl and warned him that if he left the house without a shirt and with his hair down he would get himself either arrested or raped. This induced him to wear his hair either back in a ponytail or piled on top of his head.

"At least, girl," she teased, "wear a bra. You're too sexy going around like that. I can't get my work done." But only half of this was teasing, for occasionally she would put lipstick on him and have him parade up and down before her in a pair of her Sunday heels.

"We should not drink so much," suggested Shelly on a hot day in early September.

With an askance look, "Drinking replenishes your fluids. You need to drink to live."

"We seem to drink far more alcohol than water or fruit juices."

She only shrugged and replied, "So, change that. Start drinking more water. The whole goddamn state's sitting on artesian wells, and there's more fruit juice in Florida than half the rest of the fucking world." And when he asked whether they were alcoholics, she said no they were not, but were drunkards, which was pleasantly different.

"Michael was right," he returned, "you make distinctions that normal people don't make."

She only laughed aloud and poked him with her finger. "Normal? Jesus Christmas! You're so abnormal, even Australia wouldn't want you."

"Alcohol is poison, Margie."

"Everything's poison, in a physical world."

"You're being negative on purpose."

"Because you're making yourself a victim."

He looked at her. "And what should I do about it? What's my choice?"

"You have no choice," she answered, "but to try to live and not die."

"And if I choose not to do that?"

"Then you will break my heart, and for the rest of my life I will miss you."

CHAPTER 13

December

The drive north seemed especially fatiguing to Shelly. For two days before beginning the trip he had not slept well, since hearing from his mom that his dad had had a stroke and seemed to be dying. Now, as they made their way home to see him, the inevitability of the funeral plagued him.

If the car hadn't needed servicing and winterizing for the trip, they could have left sooner. But at least now they need not worry about the car. Because of the tune-up, its engine was humming peacefully as it moved them along the winter highways and closer to Pennsylvania.

"Getting tired?" he queried, looking over at her hands as they lightly rested on the steering wheel. Her profile was so pretty, and he watched as her nose, just catching the faint dash lights, peeked from her hair. "I can drive now, if you want."

"I'm fine, just get some sleep. I'll wake you in an hour or so."

"I can't. I'm afraid of waking up in the next world."

"I said I'm fine."

"Come on, Margie, let's stop, it's the only safe thing."

"He's your dad." And with a chuckle, "If he dies before we get there, she'll be really disappointed."

"Tell the truth—she'll be fucking mad."

"So, try to get some sleep. We'll drive straight through, with just a few stops."

"She said we might hit snow."

"So? They'll clear it."

He looked out over the hood of the Olds and into the darkness. "I think he might die before we get there."

"Then, let's keep driving. Just climb in the back and try to sleep. Warm enough?"

Moving his shoulders within the thick sweater, "Yeah, it's cozy, it's perfect."

Momentarily, "Are you going to miss him?"

"I think so. Parents have to die. Whether he dies or not, I'm glad he can't run for the senate. Mom doesn't need that."

"I mean, personally. Will you miss him personally?"

The lights from the oncoming cars had given him a headache. "I don't know," he replied. "I suppose I will. It's very difficult for parents to see their child fail morally. And for Dad I think it was pretty much impossible. I think for that whole generation people like me are grotesque and deservedly the scourge of society. I couldn't help being who I was, but for him the thought of my being maybe more than half a girl was pretty much unbearable."

"When did they find out?" And when there was no response, "You don't have to tell me, of course."

He breathed a deep sigh. "No, it's fine, I don't mind. They found out when I was fourteen, actually. I simply walked into Mom's bedroom, took out her lipstick and put it on. I didn't do a very good job, which didn't end up mattering in the slightest. I looked at myself in her mirror, then just walked downstairs and sat down at the breakfast table and smiled at them. I didn't grin, I remember, but smiled. I was not trying to be confrontational."

"Good Lord! What did they do?"

"Dad nearly cried. His eyes were moist as he just sat there staring at my dark red lips."

"And your mom?"

"She sat down, put her hand on my arm, and asked if I was all right. I said that I was and asked what there was to eat. They looked at each other, then just resumed eating their breakfast. But God! You could've pushed them over with your little finger."

Clearing her throat, "I would think. So, did you keep doing it?"

"Yes, unfortunately. I also overheard them discussing whether I was a homosexual and whether or not to send me to a psychiatrist."

"And you still had short hair?"

"Yes. . . . So, every now and then, usually when they weren't home, I would put on my mom's panties and bra, her high-heeled shoes, her dresses, her jewelry. I looked really stupid. I remember how I looked in her mirror—really stupid. Anyway, they left me alone, chalking it all up to the artistic side of me, which Dad despised anyway. Mom asked me to be discreet about it and to keep it at home. She said Dad had his job to worry about."

She looked over at him. "That's really weird. I put lipstick on you and had you wear my panties, yet I didn't know any of this. Isn't that weird? I guess nature has a way of speaking whether its audience wants to listen or not."

"I didn't want to hurt them, Margie. All I knew at the time was that I wanted to wear women's clothes."

"You're so pretty now, you must have been unbelievably beautiful at about sixteen. I mean, with the lipstick and all. Did you attract guys at school?"

"I'm afraid so. I wasn't really interested in them, but yeah. I liked girls. I liked them so much I saw myself as one of them. I liked the way they walked and talked, the way they sat and crossed their legs. I liked the things they wore. Later I discovered I not only liked the feminine girls, but the masculine ones as well. They really appealed to me, I'm afraid."

"Hence me?"

"Exactly. . . . So, when did your parents find out about you?"

"When I was sixteen and in high school. I just sort of told them outright. I really didn't care what they thought about it. Actually I wasn't sensitive enough to care. Maybe if I'd considered their feelings more, I wouldn't have been so blatant. Anyway, I didn't want to hurt anybody, either. . . . I told them at dinner one evening. My mom brought in a pie and set it in the middle of the table. I remember how she cut it, gave us each a slice, then sat down. Then she asked me how things were going in school. My dad seemed interested only in his pie, so it was like I was talking just to her. On impulse, I just said to her that I was discovering that I liked both boys and girls."

"Uh-oh."

She shifted her hands, pressed the accelerator, then passed a car and returned to her lane. After checking her mirror, she continued, "You can imagine. She didn't ask me to clarify my statement. She knew what I was saying. Dad didn't, but she did. I remember how she looked at me. I had a good physique, so people could have seen me as either way. I was lifting weights a little and did definitely have ripply arms and legs. Anyway, looking at my muscles as if seeing them for the first time, she just frowned, then laughed, then said I was crazy. So—that was that."

"Uh—but there has to be more."

"Oh, there is. I had dates with boys who would ask me out. I imagine everything seemed normal to Mom. But the next year, when I was seventeen, a girl in phys-ed invited me over to study together. I stayed the night. I remember the long pause when I called Mom and told her I was staying over. . . . I didn't want to hurt anybody. I wasn't a mischievous or rebellious kid. But I did like the smell of another girl. And boy, could I smell this girl! Jesus! Anyway, later, when I brought Joey home, they were so happy. And when I married him, Mom and Dad both were almost tripping over themselves with relief."

"Then divorce, then Wellesley, then the Village and me."

"Yep."

When they reached Pennsylvania, Shelly, who had been driving for two hours, said, "It's nuts, isn't it, how far we've gone? I am so tired. Slap me, please."

"You got pretty close to that truck back there, I thought you were going to sideswipe him, which would have precluded my writing any more books and your painting the new series of nudes. So, just take it easy. I want to live to see the way your mom looks at me."

After a glance at the speedometer, he touch the power brake, then leveled off at sixty. "Isn't this a nice car, Margie?"

"It is," she agreed, with a yawn. Touching the button, she brought her window down a little to bring some fresh air into the cabin. But then closing it, she opened the wing instead. "It's big, and we both love big cars. It weighs nearly five thousand pounds, so it rides smooth as glass. And I love the power windows and seat. Yeah—it's nice."

"But it's not as nice as Sally's Eldorado, is it?"

"No. That's a hell of a lot more car than this is. All that leather, and the wire wheels—it takes real money to buy a car like that. And to Sally? It's just a big sports car to have fun with for awhile and then get tired of."

"Margie," he said after passing a pickup loaded with mattresses, "do you remember a lot from your childhood?"

"From before I told my parents?"

"Yes. I mean, about childhood things."

"I suppose I do," she answered. "Can we stop for coffee?"

"The stuff in the thermos is still hot."

Unscrewing the lid, she gave it a sniff. "Well, I remember things I wish I could forget, let's put it that way. But also some good things. You?"

"I seem to remember a lot, yes. . . . This is a really dingy highway, isn't it?"

"Like the whole world—is that what you're going to say next? Come on, cheer up."

"Who was your first kiss with?"

She chuckled. "With me. I put on red lipstick and kissed myself in the mirror."

"Well," he said, "I kissed a boy in sixth grade in the school library. I liked it. The librarian saw us and gave us both a hard slap. Then I kissed a girl, and I liked it better. Which was odd, since she didn't really kiss me back. How about you?"

She took a sip from her cup. "I didn't kiss anybody until I was sixteen. He was in my homeroom class, and we went to a movie in his dad's car. I had to kiss him. He wasn't going to do it, I could have waited all night."

"Was it nice?"

"Not really," she replied. "It was just odd. Then he drove me home, and I remember feeling like a fool. . . . But then one day I walked into a bar in Greenwich Village and sat down. Pretty soon you walked in, with your green eyes, long blond hair, your poncho, jeans, and cowboy boots, and here we are today. Yeah, I've got memories."

CHAPTER 14

It was odd for him when they finally arrived, steering the Olds up the long driveway toward the house. He could see the window of his old bedroom on the second floor, with its green awning, all, at least from the outside, as if he had never left it. Then how they got out of the car, yes, that too was odd. The very closing of the car doors seemed ominous, as did the crunching of their shoes on the salted walk, all as if communicating to them that they didn't belong here. Then trying the front door, which of course didn't open, and pushing the button above the name Byrne and hearing the muffled sound of the doorbell.

But it was odd to the point of being weird after his mother opened the door and they stepped inside, how it seemed colder inside than out. It might have been snowing in that foyer, for the chilly greeting. Even the notorious Jacksonville motorcycle cops had seemed friendlier.

"I'm Mrs. Byrne," his mother offered coldly, presenting a stiff hand to Margot. "Nice to meet you." And with the obvious absence of a hug, "Shelly, it's good to have you for a visit, even if the circumstances aren't, well, altogether pleasant. You both can hang your coats in the closet, if you wish. Otherwise, just toss them somewhere." Then she simply turned to walk away.

"Mom?" he queried.

Turning back to him, "Yes, Shelly?"

"How is he, Mom?"

Touching her puffed gray hair lightly, "He's upstairs. He's been asking for you, which is why I called. . . . Why did it take you so long to get here?"

"I'm sorry, Mom. The car needed servicing for the trip. I'm really sorry. We left as soon as we could. But how is he?"

"He's still alive, Shelly, what else can I say? I'm glad you finally got here. Please go on up. He's in the main bedroom."

At the landing, he brought a chair for Margot, then approached the door. Pulling his hair back, he drew a rubber band from his pocket, then ponytailed it and looked back at Margot. She smiled at him, and he smiled back. Then he knocked on the door and simply went in.

Leaving the door open, he stopped and looked toward the bed. His father lay covered with a mound of blankets tucked up around his chin, his gaze toward the ceiling. The lamp seemed eerily dull. Drawing his breath, he approached the bed. As he did so his father's eyes began repeatedly to blink.

"Hi, Dad," he said softly, looking down at the eyes. And when the eyes moved to look back at him, he said, "It's Shelly, Dad. Can you talk?" For some reason, it surprised him to hear a response.

"Hi, Shelly," his father said, his voice weak but clear. "Thanks for coming."

He continued to stand, as the head did not move. "It's all right, Dad, I'm here. How do you feel?"

"I'm fine, thanks, yes. Oh, Shelly, son, thanks for coming. I know it was a long way."

Reaching down, he touched the arm, then pulled the cover back and gave the hand a squeeze. "So," he said, "how's our next senator? How's things going with—" He stopped, as the eyes began to fill with tears. "Dad," he said, "it's all right. I'm here, Dad. Don't cry."

"Is she here?" he asked softly.

"Mom? Yes, just downstairs. Want me to get her?"

"No, I meant Margot. Is Margot here?"

Momentarily, "Uh, yes, Dad, sure. She's just outside, in the hall."

"Could she come in?"

"Uh, sure, Dad, okay. Just a minute."

And when he could see that Margot was standing beside the bed, too, he said, "I have something to say." Here he swallowed and began again to blink repeatedly. "Shelly, my son, and Margot, I . . . I sent the man to hurt you, to hurt you both, to—to kill you both. I was going to run for office, and I was embarrassed. . . . I—am—so—sorry!" Here he began to sob.

Slowly Shelly looked up at Margot, who was looking back at him, her face filled with shock. But then his father began again to speak.

"Will you please forgive me, Shelly? Oh, please, please forgive me, my son. And you, Margot, please forgive me. Please, I ask you both to forgive me." And again he began to sob.

After a moment, Margot said, "Mr. Byrne, I do forgive you, I do. You're at peace with me."

"Me too, Dad," said Shelly. "It's all right, everything's all right. I forgive you, too, Dad."

For a few minutes no one said anything as the two looked down at him and at each other. Gradually the crying stopped.

Then he smiled and said, his eyes going to Margot, "I hear you're quite a ball player, a hitter."

"It's just softball."

"Oh, lady," he returned, trying to give her a grin, "I think you play hardball."

Shelly looked at her and smiled. Their eyes met, then closed, for both had begun to cry. Then he looked down at his father again, but he was gone.

February 1961

Shelly set the bottle of beer upon the easel's shelf, sat down, and put his feet up on the painting table. They had just heard by phone from the lawyer that the will had been probated. Dad, his father, the would-be senator who found his ways too embarrassing to let him live, had left him and Margot $250,000 each. As the door opened he reached for the beer.

Margot, her mouth still a little open from the news, said, "You know, it's still sinking in. I just can't grasp having that much money. My God! That was so nice of him. That's a quarter of a million dollars each. That is one hell of a lot of money."

"I know," he returned. "I'm the same—I can't take it in completely. I guess I won't be able to for awhile. Dad was the man behind it all. It's just too bizarre, all of it. His sending the man to kill us, the stroke, Mom's calling us to come up, his surviving till we got there, his asking our forgiveness, and now this. It's going to take me a long time to get my equilibrium back, Margie."

Taking a seat, she looked at the blond hair, the green eyes. "What are you going to do with your money?"

"I think," he replied, with a heavy sigh, "I'll get it set up with the bank so I can live off the interest. The art world's so precarious that I cringe at the thought of trying to make a living at selling paintings. I can't teach, because I quit the Academy. And teaching isn't doing art anyway. I'm going to set mine up as a secure, steady income of some kind, even if it's not much. I want my painting to pay for itself, but God knows if that's ever going to happen. It's a sports and enter-tainment culture, not really enamored with the fine arts. And now we have this fucking Elvis Presley. That's where the money is for the arts—rock and roll."

"Well, Pollock made it all the way to *LIFE* magazine."

"Sure, as a curiosity, a freak for intellectuals to argue about. But for the average person, it's the goddamn TV set, Margie. The truth? Television is going to absolutely eat this society alive. It's not going to be long before practically all of humanity finds itself moving like shit through the bowels of television."

"Wow, thanks for the image, that's a pretty picture. I'll think of that next time I'm watching the set. Great."

He tipped the bottle and took a swig. "So, what are you going to do with your money?"

She nodded. "The same, I think."

Momentarily, "Should we combine our portions?"

She shook her head. "I'd say no. I mean, we could do it. But two accounts might be more secure than one. Any society can crucify anybody it wants to, any time it wants to. Look at what the fucking Russians and Chinese do to the people they consider undesirable. I can just see somebody like your dad deciding that we're both perverts and bringing charges against us to put us in some goddamn rehabilitation center. A society as moralistic as this one is can be as murderous as any assassin."

He finished the beer and set the bottle on the easel's shelf. Looking over into the brown eyes, he said, "Why don't we just get married, and I'll cut my hair, and we'll be legitimate? We could combine our money and live happily ever after."

"The problem there is that we'll still both be strange, and somebody might still come after us. But if we stay unmarried and keep our money separate, then if one of us is charged with something and his money confiscated, the other can use his money to rescue the first."

Wrinkling his nose, "You think that's realistic? Now you sound like the cynical one."

"Yeah, well," she replied, "I still remember Myrtle Beach, when you came into the ladies' room after you were asked to leave the men's room because of your long hair. You do realize you could have been arrested for using either restroom, right?"

"Oh, I've thought about it many times, Margie. Yeah, public restrooms have always been a problem."

"When you actually look like a woman, like you do, people are confused. This isn't Greenwich Village down here. You might want to ponytail your hair when you use the men's room. And if you have to use the ladies' room again, make sure when you go into the stall you sit to pee."

"You make it sound like we live in a war zone."

"For the most part, we do." And with a roll of her eyes, "Your dad felt he had to eliminate you so he could run for the senate. That was a massive effort. That's what society is willing to do if you get in its way. You could be more judicious in showing your feminine side. Most of the time, you wear men's clothes in public. Fine, that's great. But your hair is right out there all the time."

"You're saying I should cut my hair?"

"No, I'm not. I'm saying be judicious."

"So, I can't just wear it down?"

Exasperated, "Well, not in a goddamn police station or in a men's restroom, which is what you did. And you seem to do it a lot."

"You're picking on me. You show your muscles everywhere."

With a sigh, she hung her head. "You're right, I do. . . . God help us, Shelly."

"Well," he said, with a groan, "I don't want to think about it anymore."

She put both hands up. "Okay, so don't."

Momentarily, "Do you still like my feminine side?"

"Yes, I do. . . . But most people don't, just like they don't like my muscles."

"So, who is more repulsive, you or me?"

"Probably you. Tax payers and soldiers are still mostly men. So, yeah, probably you."

He said nothing to this, but simply looked at her. Picking up a piece of soft charcoal, he held it for a moment, then crushed it and let it fall to the floor. Running a hand along the easel's shelf, he said, "I'm ready to start the new series. Think you might have any time?"

"Sure."

"How about the new book?"

"The first draft's chugging along. I could use a break though, so now would be a good time. You'll make me notorious."

"Not unless the paintings make it to television. Besides, writers don't need artists to make them notorious. Isn't there a book-signing we have to go to?"

"In two weeks. . . . But a couple of critics haven't liked it."

"Oh, come on, Margie. Critics are the dregs, practically by definition. Even if they like you, they can't help but insult you. And their attitude of superiority and pretending to understand your art—Jesus! So, just be yourself and forget what anybody says. You have to do that anyway, or you can't write anything worth reading. You don't need me to tell you this, right?"

"Nope. But I do need to be reminded of it occasionally. Okay, let's start the picture. How about tonight?"

He looked at her. God! What a beautiful woman. There was so much to look at. Forearms like on a Michelangelo, eyes like on a Manet, flesh like on a Modigliani, and tits like on a, well, yes, a Modigliani. Finally he said, "I'll get the lamps set up."

"Oh, I forgot about dinner. That will give me a big belly, especially with beer. Maybe in the morning would be better."

But he protested, promising to make her look great, like a man with tits. And she relented, so they went down and made dinner, and had beer and dessert, and then had sex on a kitchen chair. But it was beautiful, or at least, as they said, they perceived it to be so.

CHAPTER 15

"Now see there," she said later, finding a comfortable place amid the cushions on   the overstuffed chair, "just like I said—my stomach is bulging with dinner and beer." And settling herself in and taking up the book that was to be her prop, "Why did I drink the fucking beer?"

Ignoring this, he shifted the main easel to clear his view of the scene. It was a ritual, and he didn't want to rush things. It was like making love, where the point of it all was not so much in the achievement as in the experience. Placing the canvas on the easel's shelf, he sat down, broke off a piece of soft charcoal, and looked at the scene.

"That's a pretty small canvas," she said, looking up from the book.

"Don't complain. It's perfect. Twenty-by-sixteen is an intimate size for a painting, very appropriate for a nude. What do you want, the whole wall?"

"No. but something with footage, at least."

"Yeah, well, that might get us arrested."

"Then, just abstract it."

"This is not going to be an abstract, Margie. They're going to be able to smell the woman in this one. So, any bigger, yeah, the penitentiary. . . . You're not cold, are you? I turned the heat up before we ate, and I think it's about eighty in here. But it's your nipples, so if you're not comfortable, speak up. It's going to take about an hour and a half for this sitting."

"I'm fine for now. But go—let me hear that charcoal moving, girl. But my stomach's like a goddamn watermelon."

He looked at the scene again. "Lower the book. Let your arm rest on the chair. . . . Perfect. Now pull the glasses down just a smidge. . . . Yep, that's it, I think. Now, don't move."

"I'm going to have to push the glasses up occasionally. If you'd just let me wear mine they wouldn't keep slipping down."

"Sorry. I like these. I've always gotten the props I could afford."

"Well, at least that can change, with all that money. . . . Shelly, maybe I should cross my legs. I think I need a shower from our little kitchen chair incident."

"No, don't move, I said. What's wrong with you? I'm the one who sets things up, not you."

As the scratching of the charcoal began to sound, Margot, her eyes upon the book, said, "For the next session, I would like to have music."

"I'll have it ready. What would you like?"

"Ravel would be nice. Or maybe a Bruckner symphony, if the next session's going to be an hour and a half, too."

"We need another hi-fi set, maybe two more. You should have one for your studio, and I'd like one in here. They're cheap enough, we shouldn't have to lug it up and down the stairs."

"We'll have to lug the records back and forth anyway. You're lazy, Shelly. Do you still like Bruckner?"

A sigh. "Yes. It's the most beautiful music, I think. I have an emotional connection with every symphony except the last. And that's only because he didn't finish it. Hey, you've looked up."

"Sorry."

"That's all right. This is very nice. Thanks for sitting for me."

"What are you going to call it?"

"Maybe *Margot Reading In A Chair*. How does that sound?"

"Shouldn't that be *on* a chair. One sits on a chair."

He stopped to consider this. "No. It's an overstuffed chair, and your ass is definitely down in it."

"Going to put my name in the title this time, huh?"

"Why not?" he replied. "By the way, I've reread your book. I still see myself as Amy Roche."

She looked up from the book. "But she's sexless. And you're not sexless, sweetheart."

He smiled. "No," he returned, pulling a brush from the oil jar, "but I do like Bruckner. Maybe that counts."

After wiping the small sable, he laid it aside and reached for the tin cup. He squeezed a tiny portion of burnt sienna into it and then added a small portion of turpentine. After first touching the brush to the paint, then dipping it into the liquid, he began to turp-in the charcoal outline. For him, going through this process was, yes, like listening to Bruckner. It was a ritual, something done over and over until it was so familiar it must be repeated for sheer peace of soul.

"Hey," she said suddenly, "I seem to be losing you. Are you dreaming?"

"Just concentrating. Don't mess with me."

"So—what do you think about Kennedy?"

"Please, Margie, no politics. I hate politics."

"I know. But do you think he could be on our side?"

"Our? What does that mean?"

"You know—strange people."

"Oh God, Margie. Really? I can't believe you're asking me that. If you think any of these goofy politicians gives a fuck about anybody on the face of the earth, you're naïve."

"I know. But I mean *overtly* on our side."

He gave her a look, then went back to the picture. "You're forgetting your definitions," he said as he worked. "You should look up *politician* again. A politician, no matter which party he claims to represent, isn't just a hypocrite, but a professional one, someone who is actually paid by the people to be one. Politicians sell you the idea that they're on your side, while ironically, they're all just sellouts. They're great in the pulpit, but trade their message in for a better deal in the back room. You hope in them, that they'll represent your cause, and they swear to God almighty they will. So, you entrust them with your cause. Then, after they've taken your money and your heart, they take a shit on your cause. No, I don't care for politicians or politics. I'll gladly leave them to the poor fuckingly naïve idealists, like Michael."

"Whew! That was harsh. But, well said."

"Sorry."

"No, no, don't apologize. ... But you don't believe in the people either."

"The *people*? Jesus God, Margie! The people? Really? Let's see, what do the people do? Their main purpose, if you can call it that, seems to be to make babies, money and wars. Oh, and of course occasionally to demand the crucifixion of a Christ or two."

"And you see society as what?"

He looked up from the picture, then at the ceiling, then said, "Let's see, how would I define society? I think I would say that it's the general body of the community expressed as a force. It's a beast, like the Beast in Revelation, which I think is a kind of fantastically big political system. But yeah, I think society's a beast."

"Wonderful. So, why am I writing and why are you painting? To help this awful beast?"

He smiled, as if to himself and to home in on the truth. "I don't know what you do it for, but I do it for sex and alcohol."

"And Pollock—what would you say he did it for?"

With a shrug, "Just the alcohol."

"Did you ever think about taking drugs?"

"No."

"You're a weird one, Miss Byrne, even weirder than I am. But I love that about you."

"You like calling me *miss* and *girl*, don't you?"

With a coy look, "I do. It's sexy."

"So," he said, adjusting the level of the shelf, "we fit together well, would you say?"

"I would say we balance each other out." And giving her nose a scratch, "You're too cynical for me, dear, which is so ironic it's bizarre. You say you're the soft one, and I'm the hard one who can kill a man, I'm the one with muscles, and all that. But you're the one who is hard on society. I'm the one who is soft on society, and who writes about hope. But I like your description of a politician as a professional hypocrite. That's very good. Can I use it?"

He chuckled. "Why would you ask? It's certainly not original. So, will you share your Nobel Prize with me?"

"Whew! I can't imagine what you think of such a construct when it comes to the arts. But I'm sure I will share it, if I ever get it—at least, I'll share the money. I've shared my bed with you, I might as well share my Nobel Prize too."

He stuck the brush into the oil jar. "Someday people are going to argue as to whether this painting is more about you or about me. They'll say, 'S. Byrne may have put the paint on, but Margot Bernard's the one we see'."

Laying the book aside and arching her back, "And they'll fall in love with you as one of my characters. But they'll also see me back there, typing away." And getting up, "I think we'll share in each other's glory, if there's any to share in."

With a heavy sigh, "Sure, why not? We're each other's muse. What can go wrong?"

CHAPTER 16

As he drove through Five Points on his way home Shelly felt a peace come over him. Just telling Detective Tipper about his dad's confession had seemed to bring a certain finality to it all. But Tipper had been reluctant to express satisfaction that the plot had come to a close. In his experience, he said, plots could be quite complex, multi-faceted, and could easily produce insidious and tenacious subplots. However, the detective had been quite relieved to hear that at least the person and motive behind it all had been identified.

Accelerating from an intersection, he glanced to his right, at the old church where Margot and he often went swimming in the indoor pool, avoiding of course Saturdays, when all the kids were there. Then, ahead but also to his right, he saw the convent. Entering Two Points, he made a left at the light and drove down King toward the river.

After crossing Riverside, he made a left onto Harris, then swung right into the driveway.

Leaving the windows down, he switched off and withdrew the key from the ignition. For a moment he sat listening to the tinkling of the car as it began rapidly to cool. Before meeting Margot he had often wondered why cars made such odd sounds. She had taught him and helped him so much! If he painted a hundred years, he could not express how much she had accepted him and loved him.

Running a hand through his hair, he pulled the mirror over and looked at himself. He looked pale. The green of the eyes seemed lighter than usual, and the lips, which he felt needed a little color, seemed especially lackluster. He had never understood why people made such a fuss when a man simply put on a little lipstick. Nevertheless the complaint was there in force, so he never wore it out in public. Yes, he looked especially pale today, but still he looked pretty. Then he pushed the mirror back, got out, and went inside.

Pushing her door open, he leaned against the doorframe and simply looked at her, as if for sympathy.

Rolling her chair back, she met his eyes. "What did he say? Probably a lot of bullshit, right?"

With a sigh, "Not exactly. He seemed relieved to at least understand who had been behind it all. And he said we should still stay alert for what he called subplots and for other people who might still be coming after us."

She brought her foot to her knee. "How did he take your explanation of why your dad found you so embarassing?"

"Well," he returned, closing his eyes, "he didn't seem interested in any details. Staring at my hair and looking me up and down the whole time, he simply said he understood. God! It was so awkward!"

"Which is understandable," she returned a little sarcastically.

Opening his eyes, "Yes, it is."

"I mean, you could always cut your hair and blend in like most other people do."

He nodded, but looked down.

"But you don't," she continued. "And I like that about you. I wouldn't change a thing about you, except maybe to ponytail your hair for certain occasions, as a compromise. But ... let's be honest, people have a right to their fucking opinion."

"You're right."

"Then, no complaints? I mean, the guy's done so much for us."

"No complaints."

"Peace?"

Nodding, "Peace."

The time until the book-signing seemed to pass much more quickly than Margot had wished. Even on the morning of the event she felt unprepared. For all of Shelly's attempts to put her at ease and reassure her that she was ready to present and defend her work, still she worried so much that her stomach hurt. Even filling herself with a huge bowl of cold cereal and milk did not help.

The proprietor of Kranston's Books, pleasant and unassuming, had assured her that only a brief oral summary of the book was necessary, followed of course by the answering of any questions from the audience. For the rest of the afternoon it would only be necessary to sit behind a table and sign the books as patrons brought them to her.

At the store they were greeted by the manager, a plump woman in her sixties, who stood before Margot as if to do homage. Her hair, unnaturally black, had been pinned up in a pile on top of her head. A pink plastic-covered nameplate had been fixed to her lapel.

"I enjoy the signings so much," she cooed. "Over thirty people responded to the invitations, and I'm sure others will see the sign out front and your book in the window and wish to come in."

It was thirty minutes later that Margot finished her summary and stood waiting for questions. The first came from a man on the second row.

"How do you write?" he asked.

"Uh," she began, with a few blinks, "well, every writer has a favorite way of arranging the paper, the desk, all of it. I usually write with a cup of tea close by."

When the general chuckling died, he said meekly, "No, I mean, how do you come up with ideas, stories? Because when I try to write I get a whole idea, but my typing is really slow compared to my thinking."

She shifted her weight onto the other foot. "Personally I simply write as I type. I type a few words and then see where it leads me. Many writers, of course, choose to hold off on the actual physical writing of the story until they get a general plot and characters in mind. Then they make a few notes, an outline of the story, and a short list of plausible characters. Then they start the actual writing and follow the notes and outline. Does that help?"

"Sure, yeah. Thanks."

Then a formidable-looking woman on the front row straightened herself and said, "As a librarian I was wondering whether you anticipate problems getting your book accepted at public libraries."

For a moment Margot simply looked at the woman. There was certainly a malignancy in the tone. Then, instead of playing coy, she decided to just meet the thing head on. Clearing her throat, she queried, "Did you find the book to be offensive?"

The woman also cleared her throat. "No," she returned, "not exactly. But one of the main characters did exhibit morally questionable behavior when he wore women's clothes to the party near the end of the book."

With a nod, to at once acknowledge the obvious criticism yet avoid playing coy, she said, "Uh-huh. So, you see that as a problem subject to write about?"

"Well, certainly, if a writer includes such a subject in his book at all, he must do it with the utmost delicacy."

"And would you say that I have done that?"

Hesitating, "Not entirely, no."

Margot brought her hands together on the podium. "How so?"

"Well," returned the woman, straightening her position on the chair, "you did not, within the book, excoriate the behavior or even put it in a bad light. When an author writes a book, especially one of fiction, he is making a social statement. So, by not condemning immoral behavior he glorifies it."

"By simply dealing with it?"

Emphatically, and with some severity, "Correct. As a matter of fact, he does so especially when he makes that character in the story to be charming in other ways. Which, of course, you have done in your story."

Margot looked at the smiling but clearly frightened face of the manager, who from a seat on the back row had been following the discussion closely. Then she looked around at the other attendants, all of whom appeared to be awaiting her answer. Then she looked over at Shelly. Then she spoke.

"But what if the writer is not so much a moralist as a realist? What if the writer means to do something other than simply comment on or even parrot the mores of society? For instance, what if the writer is an existentialist and wishes to deal with authenticity. Or what if the writer is a very spiritual person and wishes to deal with matters of love, honor, truth, beauty?"

Now the woman sat forward on the chair. "Any writer, especially a writer of fiction, must work within the confines of the moral standards of his society, or risk being rejected by the moral members of that society."

"Such as those who run the libraries?"

The woman nearly audibly gritted her teeth at this, but then replied icily, "Correct. Moral people can affect not only what their children read, such as at a school or library, but to some extent what the public reads, such as materials from bookstores."

Now the manager simply turned red and looked down.

Lifting her chin a little, Margot said, "Does anyone else have a question?"

For a few moments there was a palpable silence. Then a man seated near Shelly raised his hand, then said, "I noticed while reading your book an overall atmosphere of hope. And when I had finished it I couldn't help thinking that this author must be a person of immense hope. Was I wrong, are you a hopeful person, or do you tend to be more cynical—I mean, in your everyday life?"

"No, you were correct. I have a tendency to come down on the side of hope."

"Would you say that's a right perspective on life? Do you think we should all be more hopeful?"

"Well, I'm not a moralist, so I wouldn't venture a judgment that being hopeful is either right or wrong. And again, I don't usually think in terms of what we should do, but more in terms of what we actually do. . . . Could I ask, did you have a favorite character in the story, and if so, who?"

He folded his arms defensively, but smiled. "Actually," he replied, "I think I liked the man that wore the high heels to the party. It seemed that he was honest in saying he didn't know who he was inside, while some of the people around him didn't know who they were either, but weren't so honest in admitting it. I don't know, he just impressed me as someone seeking the truth rather than just the approval of his peers."

She nodded, then smiled, then noticed he was smiling back at her. She also noticed that Shelly's eyes had become moist and that the manager was no longer looking down, but up.

CHAPTER 17

The Bonnie Henney Fine Art Gallery in downtown Jacksonville, one of the three most reputable galleries south of Atlanta and north of Miami, had been in existence for only ten years, opening in 1950. During its first six years, its owner and director had intentionally carried only representational art. But when Jackson Pollock died in August 1956, she experienced not only a change of heart, as she herself later put it, but a change of aesthetic perspective as well. Since the painter's death she had opened the gallery's doors to include not only works by artists of the New York School, but all twentieth century abstract art. And by 1961 she herself had actually come to prefer modern over traditional art.

Bonnie Henney had left New York and come south following her husband's death from cancer in 1950. Her intention had been not only to find a new life for herself, away from what she called the grotesque physical as well as emotional coldness of Manhattan, but to spend that life forwarding the careers of fresh talent. To say the least, she had been successful, so that now, at only fifty-two, she could already boast of helping to forward the careers of numerous nationally recognized artists. Guided by her own aesthetic eye and dictatorial business sense, she had built a reputation so trustworthy that collectors from all over the country sought her advice when making their art purchases, and artists practically killed each other for a chance to win her favor. In short, for collector and artist alike, her word had become pure gold.

As Shelly and Margot entered the gallery they were relieved that they had chosen to dress more up than down. Everything from floor to ceiling, especially the art, emanated professionalism. For Shelly, the contrast between the meticulously crafted appearance here and the shabby, even sometimes dingy, appearance of the Greenwich Village galleries was striking.

"No flip-flops here," muttered Margot, with a roll of her eyes.

As they set down the paintings they had been carrying a woman seated at an immaculate desk got up. "Hello," she said, giving her horn-rimmed glasses a push. "Can I help you?"

"Yes, I'm Shelly Byrne and this is Margot Bernard. I called about presenting some of my work. I spoke with Bonnie Henney."

"Yes, of course. I'm Tricia. Nice to meet you both. Bonnie's working upstairs with the framers. I'll tell her you're here. Feel free to look around." And as she walked away she turned, as if knowing that they had looked at the name plate on the desk, and said, "Tricia Sweat—pronounced just like the perspiration. I'll be back in a moment."

As she walked away Margot watched the high-heeled shoes, the black slacks, the tight top. "That," she whispered, "is a nice piece of ass. Did you see the skin? Like milk, right? And the hair—God, I love blonds!"

Shelly, however, his eyes taking in the hanging art, did not respond. Most of the work, he noted, was representational. But at least one third of it was abstract, and some of these, completely nonobjective. All the pieces had been exquisitely framed. There did not appear to be any sculpture in the gallery.

"Did you see," continued Margot, "the low-cut shirt? You weren't even looking."

Suddenly Tricia and another woman emerged from a doorway at the rear of the gallery and walked toward them. If Tricia walked with an unmistakable sensuality, the other woman, in a black silk top, tight taupe slacks, and high-heeled sandals, carried herself with a certain sensuous dignity—a dignity tempered, however, by a half-full glass of something on the rocks. Further, she held the drink as if to say it was intrinsic to her personality.

"Hello," said the woman cordially, without waiting to be introduced, "I'm Bonnie, the director." And extending her free hand, "You must be Shelly, and you're Margot. It's very nice to meet you both." Then she raised the glass, took a hefty drink from it, and said, "You've met Tricia here. She and I will take a look at your things. I'm so glad you could bring in the actual work and not just photographs—or even send them by mail. That's rustic, if you ask me. I mean, what am I supposed to do? I can't just look at some photograph and go, 'oh, look at this, a great work of art,' can I? I mean, I try to be sensitive, but I don't have a crystal ball. I need to see the work, like anybody else, right? I need to see it in order to feel it. Does that make sense to you? Does it?"

Shelly, taken somewhat aback by the assertive personality, for a moment merely stared at the woman. He could not resist wondering how the immaculate skin, the pretty brunette hair, the seemingly perfectly proportioned body, might paint up as a nude. "Uh—yes," he replied at length. "Yes, it does."

Henney, who had followed up the little tirade by taking a drink from the glass, then queried, "Would either of you care for a drink? I'm having gin, but we can get you something else. A little scotch?"

Shelly, after trying in vain to fit the immaculate appearance to the powerful smell of alcohol, simply met the intense gray eyes and replied, "I'm, uh, I'm fine, thanks."

But not to let it go, Henney repeated the query with a simple raise of her eyebrows in Margot's direction.

Margot, wondering how to use both the woman and Tricia as characters in her new book, eventually chimed that she too was fine.

"Well," said Henney, "I don't myself drink, at least not very much, and especially not this early in the day, but I was becoming a little parched."

Neither Shelly nor Margot replied to this, but Tricia cleared her throat delicately, as if in unbelief over an audacious lie.

Henney, her eyes fixed for a moment upon Shelly's glamorous hair, glanced at the paintings, then merely smiled and continued. "I hope it wasn't a lot of trouble to bring them in."

"Oh, not at all," he replied. "We live in the Riverside area."

"Yes, I know you do," she returned, with a definite frankness. "And I know who you are, too. You're the two who had the intruder some while ago, aren't you?"

This time it was Margot who cleared her throat, wondering whether the woman ever pitched straight or only threw curveballs. But she said nothing, leaving the question for Shelly to answer.

"Yes," he replied at length, his eyes moving down the expensive clothes to the bare ankles, the Riviera-looking shoes, "that's correct."

"You beat the poor soul to death, I understand." But with the smile again, "I'm kidding. He got what he deserved, if you ask me." And to Margot, "If I recall from the article, you're the one who did it?"

Margot cocked her head, then replied, "I am."

"Well, my husband, while he was alive, of course, would have been the first to applaud you. He hated crime. Most wealthy people hate crime, at least vulgar crime, I suppose. But that's another subject." And taking in the solid biceps and triceps, "You seem very athletic. I'll bet you look great in a swimsuit."

"Actually I'm a writer. But yeah, I get a lot of exercise."

With her eyes fixed upon the rocky arms, "Nobody gets muscles like that sitting behind a typewriter."

Delicately Tricia cleared her throat again. "Uh, Bonnie?"

"What? Oh, yes. Sorry. All right, so, ladies, what do you have to show me here? Let's spread them out so we can get some good light on them."

When the paintings had been sufficiently spread out, she simply made a single pass in front of them, then said, "These were all done with a knife. Do you ever use other tools?"

After nearly holding his breath, he replied, "Yes. But I generally use the same kind of tools for a particular kind of painting. For representational landscapes I usually use a flat white bristle. For these spatial pieces, nearly always a knife."

"So, you would not mix knife and brush in the same painting?"

"No."

"These look like oil, and just with linseed and maybe a little varnish for spreading, except for those two, where you probably used some turp to get the wash."

"Correct."

Suddenly the woman turned, walked about fifteen feet away, and stood looking at the whole group of paintings. Taking an occasional drink from the glass, she said nothing for a moment or two. Then she took a larger drink, rolled it around in her mouth, swallowed slowly, and said, "Tricia, what do you think?"

The other shrugged. "They're very nice."

"So, we can sell them?"

"I would think so, yes."

"Okay," said Henney, with a nod. "Okay. Well, Shelly, I like them. I'm glad you just brought abstracts. Anything else would be confusing, at this point. I don't sell many abstracts, but some. How much do you want for them?"

"Two hundred for the 24-by-30's, three hundred for the 28-by-36's."

Momentarily, "That sounds good. I'll double it, of course, so they'll be priced at four and six hundred without frames. . . . Tricia? Frames?"

The response was nearly beautiful, Shelly thought, as Tricia for a moment said nothing, but then, lifting her chin and moving like a cat, walked over to stand beside Henney. Margot too watched, as if mesmerized by the sultry, nearly dramatic movements of the still silent woman.

"Probably," said Tricia at length, "the simple black satin. And with the two dark ones, probably the same in white."

"Oh, I agree," chimed the other a fraction of a second later. "Okay, Shelly, I'll frame all of them and hang, oh, probably five. I'll call my collectors and have them take a look. No one-man show, yet, you understand. But I'll show them, and we'll make sure everybody that comes in sees them. I have one elderly couple from Atlanta and a young guy from Miami who collect nonobjective art. I have collectors from all over actually." And giving Tricia a nod, "Call them. Oh, and get a picture of one of these in the Times Union article for next Sunday. Let's give this stuff some exposure." And to Shelly, "Then, if it sells—I mean even if I sell only half of these right here—well, then we'll do a show. You do have others like these, right?"

He blinked, as if a little overwhelmed. "I have a lot of them actually."

"Good. . . . So, what are your thoughts? Go ahead, just tell me straight out. What do you think? And you too, Margot." Here she let her eyes followed the muscles again. "Don't hold back. I want to hear what both of you think."

Shelly drew his breath. "Uh, I think it all sounds good, very good. Yeah, sure."

"Wonderful." And after taking another drink, "Margot, your thoughts?"

Although she could not help taking a moment to watch more of the alcohol theater play out as Henney took another hefty drink from the glass, Margot, as if to bring herself into a more practical frame of mind, forced herself to look away, then asked, "What happens if they don't sell?"

"Then we'll try some of the other things. I like this work so much, that I'm sure there are other pieces we can try."

"And the cost of the framing? How will that be recovered?"

It was Tricia who answered, and in a tone that said the question had been mundane. "We'll absorb it, that's all. Don't worry about that."

"Are you two sure," said Henney, giving the ice in her glass a gentle shake, "you wouldn't like a drink? We have plenty of ice and anything you want."

"I'm fine," returned Shelly, squinting a little.

When Margot again chimed the same, Henney glanced at her watch, then said, "I have to run now, I'm afraid, as I'm working with the framer. Next time you come we'll all have to go out for drinks and some lunch—that would be chummy. It was nice to meet both of you." Then she shook their hands, holding on a little longer to Margot's, as if to feel the grip. "Tricia will give you a consignment agreement to take with you. It was so pleasant to meet you both, and we're glad to have you with us."

And turning, she walked away, but not without throwing them a little wave over her shoulder.

CHAPTER 18

The highway that led to Jacksonville Beach was mostly straight. On a good day Margot knew she could make the trip from the city to the beach in eighteen minutes. Today she was shooting for seventeen. After crossing the bridge and clearing the city, she put her foot down, and the 98's Hydramatic blew down into second as the Rocket V8 roared.

Tripping the switch, she brought her window nearly to the top, then said, "Help me look for cops. God! This thing's fast."

"You don't want to kill us," Shelly returned, his eyes scanning the roadside for lurking cruisers of the Highway Patrol."

Bringing the power seat up to give them a better view of the highway, she merely grinned and waited for the Hydramatic to hit fourth. "Why not?" she said, "I'll make you famous. Pollock number two, here we go."

He leaned over to read the speedometer. "We're going eighty . . . ninety. Slow down, would you? If we go any faster, they'll think we're a U-2."

"And try to shoot us down?" But lifting her foot, she backed them down to seventy-five and settled in for the ride. The correction to the pace would not be without its advantages. At the least, it might free her mind a little to consider one or two of the problem characters in the new book.

"They shouldn't let people like you play with cars or guns or girls," he said after a minute or so had passed. "How fast are you going now?"

"Come on, Shelly, seventy-five. Don't wet your panties."

"Yeah, well, I've seen it before. You can get maniacal behind the wheel."

"Do you like this car? Tell the truth."

"I do. But I loved Sally's Eldorado. For me, Margie, that was a sexy car."

"So, buy one. You can afford it now."

"And what's your favorite car?"

"I guess I like the XK150."

"That's a Jaguar?"

"It is. It's gorgeous, fast, and has a lot of class."

"How much?"

"More than ten thousand, I think. And now you're going to tell me to buy one, right? No, I'm not buying one."

For a few minutes they simply listened to the wind blowing over the wing vents. Closing his, Shelly queried, "Would you consider Sally to have class?"

"I suppose. If she doesn't, she's certainly got enough money to fake it."

"Michael's kind of pathetic, isn't he? I mean, the typical idealist."

"Yep." But then, with an audible sigh, "Which is something nobody will ever call you, that's for sure. Jesus!"

"Pathetic?"

"No, an idealist. You are so cynical, Shelly! I have often wondered why you're that way."

He ran a hand through his hair, then flipped the visor down and looked at himself in the mirror. "Maybe having a father like mine, I don't know."

She winced. "That's bullshit! That whole cause-and-effect thing is pure bullshit. At least, I think it is. People who see life that way see themselves as victims, that they are who they are because of either what has happened to them, or the way they were raised, or even just the way they were born. I've never been able to buy into that kind of thinking. The human mind is too powerful and independent, and enables a person to overcome just about any obstacle."

Flipping the visor up again, "I know. You've told me before all about it—individuals are responsible for their actions. I know, I know, I know. So, please, not again."

"Well," she returned, "what do you expect when you say that having a father like yours has made you think the way you do? Really?"

He grabbed a handful of hair and pushed it behind his ear. "To a certain extent it has, I think."

Giving the wheel a little slap, "That's totally illogical. Your father didn't make you wear your hair long. He actually tried to kill you because of your long hair, among other things."

"It's still all related. That's all I'm saying. Maybe I let my hair grow either positively or negatively because of my father. You don't know, and maybe even I don't know. Not everything is overt, conscious, and a product of cause and effect. Everything's related. Maybe people are responsible, but to a certain extent they're not. And, I know, you disagree. You've preached it before."

"I don't entirely disagree. Sure, everything's related, but not to the extent you think they are. Otherwise there couldn't be laws, or retribution or reward, or even God. We don't need to fight about it. I emphasize responsibility, and you emphasize influence."

"I do emphasize it," he returned, "because that's what I see all around me. I think you can prove that cause and effect is powerful in forming every personality. Everything from chemicals to society helps to make people who they are. And if some effect happens, well, then responsibility of the individual is no longer a qualitative thing, but a quantitative thing. Furthermore, to make the individual qualitatively responsible is to give him the power of God in his own life. But then, how would he be able to call out for mercy or be aware of his own moral failure?"

"My emphasis," she replied, "will always come down on the responsibility side. People are more active than passive. They're not so much victims as they are free and have the power to be who and what they want to be."

"Okay, okay. Let's just stop with it, okay? Christmas! I don't really fucking care anyway."

She moved them into the passing lane, then accelerated past a truck. "So, why did you ask if Sally had class?"

"Because she called this afternoon. She's breaking up with Michael."

"Jeez, Shelly, why didn't you tell me?"

"Sorry. I was concentrating on getting my stuff together."

"So, what reason did she give?"

"She said she just looked at his pathetic face one morning over breakfast and decided she couldn't see a future for them. She said she finished her eggs, then her coffee, then just told him straight out that she didn't care about any of his ideas about the world. She told him all she cared about in life was enjoying herself."

"And? Come on, Shelly, don't tease, tell me everything she said."

"She said she didn't even give him a chance to respond. She told him she didn't care about the poor or workers' rights or war or any other of his grand concerns, and wasn't about to join him on any goddamn picket line. And then told him she didn't care about politics in the slightest, at which point, she said, he simply began to cry."

She puffed her cheeks. "Poor guy! Damn! That's big, that's atomic. I didn't think it would last. Talk about social opposites. I like her, but she is a bit empty. I don't feel sorry for her. I envy her a little. But Michael? No, I don't envy him. He can't seem to figure out which is more important to him, his mind or his body. Sally's a really pretty girl. I can see how sniffing after her money-pampered ass and following his ideals might get him confused."

"Well," he continued, "I haven't told you the biggest news of all. I mean, hold on tight, Margie. She said to me right on the phone that, just between her and us, she's looking for another kind of relationship."

"Oh."

"Right, Margie? Big, right?" And pulling the visor down again, he looked at himself, then pushed it back up.

"Want some lipstick?"

Ignoring this, he continued, "That's the problem with nature attracting opposites. Sally and Michael, would have been, what, nature's choice? What is it with nature? Does it attract opposites so that each can provide a correcting perspective? Is it all just chemistry, like for getting the best kids out of you? You would think nature would match you. Instead it seems to deliberately mismatch you."

"You're right," she returned, "but you can't think about it too much."

"But nature isn't malicious, it's simply doing the population thing. So, when it gets the kids out of you, and they go off to college or get married, and you only have each other to live with every day, you turn to hating each other. Every couple out there seems to do that. You hate each other because you're opposites and never really cared for each other anyway. But society pays you to keep the marriage together, so you turn to hobbies and anything else you can think of so you don't have to be with the other person more than is bearable. And nature doesn't care, because it can't get any more kids out of you."

"Shelly, you're thinking too much about it. Why torture yourself?"

"Because we're opposites, in so many ways. You have a defense mentality, I don't. You practically seek confrontation, I avoid it. You seem to enjoy a fight, I find fighting disgusting. You're hard, I'm soft. You're strong, I'm weak. You have a strong smell, I have no smell at all. You have hair under your arms, I have nothing under my arms. And psychologically we have different architecture, anyone can see it."

CHAPTER 19

They had worn street clothes over their swimsuits, thinking to assess the situation before making a commitment. After they had parked, they gave each other a look of solidarity, then got out and walked the block and a half to the beach.

The seemingly endless white sand of Jax Beach lay hot as a desert as they stepped from the walkway and began to make their way toward the water. But between them and the breakers was a line of cars parked on the sand and facing the ocean, all as if parked at a drive-in movie. But the real show was neither the endless line of parked cars nor the glorious greenish breakers foaming in from the ocean, but the parade of bikinied women and men walking the beach at the water's edge.

"God! Look at them!" exclaimed Shelly as they stretched out the blanket over the spot they had chosen. "Tell me what I'm looking at, please."

Margot pushed her sunglasses up. "How about hundreds, or maybe thousands, of nearly naked people? Don't pee yourself, girl. You're an artist, you're used to the flesh." And dropping her shorts, then removing her top, she said, "This is my first bikini—and it may be my last. Don't tell me how naked I feel."

"Just be glad," he said, "you're not carrying a gun everywhere now. Where would you put it?"

"Well, yours is like a rubber band," she came back, giving him the eye. "Let's just say, I can sure see your balls, ma'am."

Not far away a powder-blue Cadillac, its top down, was being backed into a space. Even before the tanned teenaged boy shut the engine down the blond, bikinied girl beside him, who had been riding up on the door's edge, put her leg over the side and slipped to the sand. The boy and girl in the back seat, who had been riding up on the car with their feet on the seat, also jumped out. Switching off, the driver swung his door open, got out, and stood, bronzed and barefoot, watching while the others pulled a blanket from the trunk, then spread it out behind the car.

"I guess," said Shelly, "it's that Coppertone shit that gets them like that. I wonder what else it does to them."

She was stretching out on the blanket. "Hey," she said, "want to go up there and get something to drink? I'm kind of hot. And we can get something to eat too, if you want."

But he simply continued watching, his eyes moving from blanket to blanket as people sunbathed, then out to the flat part of the beach near the water, where, displaying their physical equipment, a long stream of bikinied girls and a few boys walked. Nearby an attractive, darkly tanned girl with long brown hair lay waiting as her boyfriend stubbed his cigarette into the sand, then began to rub lotion onto her stomach. Everything—the sand, the cars, the umbrellas and blankets, even the people—all seemed to glow, as if receiving the light and heat of a slowly exploding nuclear bomb.

"Hey!" said Margot again, to get his attention. "What are you looking at, the flesh parade? How about it, want to go get something to drink? How about a cold beer?"

Looking down at her, he replied, "As Bonnie would say, I don't really drink, but I don't want to get parched. So, let's go see what we can find." And taking her hand, he pulled her up. Bringing her close, he kissed her, but could not see her eyes behind the dark glasses. Suddenly aware that people were watching, he let go of her hand and simply asked if they could start walking.

Mischievously she replied, "So, you don't think we should stand here in front of the whole beach and show our affection for each other?"

He did not answer, but merely slipped his sunglasses on, then ran both hands through his hair, fluffing it out as it ran past his shoulders. Margot was not alone in watching him do this, for a number of heads turned, and a woman not far way pulled her sunglasses down to get a better look and, apparently upset, said something to the man who was with her.

"God! You are so pretty!" said Margot. "People are watching, you know. They think we're lesbians and you left the top half of your bikini in the car. I think I'm going to get you a top half in one of these shops, just to feed their suspicions."

"Then I *will* have to use the ladies' room."

"That's right," she replied, with a chuckle, "and sit to pee."

With a smile, he put his hand out and took hers again. "Come on," he said softly, "let's walk."

Returning the smile, she gave his hand a squeeze. With heads turning and eyes following them, it seemed, from every nearby blanket, they left their things and, hand in hand, began to make their way toward the boardwalk area.

Later, while driving through the darkness back to Jacksonville, Shelly said, "I can't believe you did that."

"Why? If I can wear men's clothes, why can't you wear women's."

"You actually bought a bikini top and had me wear it."

"And we went to the ladies' room together, and no one said a thing or even looked at us. And when we rinsed the sand from our ankles those men whistled at you."

"That's because you had me put on lipstick."

"But it was fun, right?"

"Not really," he said, "the bottom was too tight."

"I'll get you one that isn't, don't worry about it. I'm telling you, I'm going to make you really totally believable. Fun, right?"

"But that aside," he said, "you know, I think my romance with the beach may have come to its logical end. I don't mind being part of the flesh parade and all that, but I don't like getting cooked at the same time."

"Well, honey sweets," she returned, leaning over to kiss his arm, "you gave me a real hard-on. I had a really fun day. But yeah, I know what you're saying. I think I got burned."

"People always do."

She reached to feel her burned toes. "But," she said, "I'm keeping the bikini. It was erotic just wearing it. I wonder what a nude beach would be like."

"They're in France, right? We should go. I'd love it. I'll take a camera."

"But it was fun, right? We'll have to go back. And we'll park out on the beach."

He did not answer, but simply continued to look out over the hood at the traffic. Just ahead a big Chevrolet station wagon loaded with a large group careened as the woman in the passenger seat passed food back to children. Suddenly the woman took something from the man driving, cranked her window down, and threw it out. Why the whole scene seemed normal Shelly did not know. Perhaps because he could almost see Dad driving and Mom beside him as he watched them from the back seat.

"Margie," he said at length, "what's wrong with us?"

"Everything," she answered. But when there was no response, she said, "I'm just kidding. I'm not sure we actually have a lot wrong with us. It's just such a shitty world. Don't you go to the movies?"

"I do," he returned. "I go with my girlfriend, who writes books full of hope for hopeless people."

Suddenly the woman in the station wagon, who apparently had been collecting trash from the others, rolled her window down and shoved it all out. Instantly it was blown into parts. Paper cups, napkins, and food were carried back over the hood of the Olds.

"Look at that!" exclaimed Margot. "Is that gross, or what? How could she do that? I suppose they're going to urinate out the window next."

"Maybe she knows it's a shitty world already, and it doesn't matter what she throws out the window."

She looked at him. "Don't be negative, Miss Byrne, I don't want to hear it. ... Look, she's going to throw more out. I hope a cop sees her."

The highway seemed aglow with red taillights as they moved with the returning crowds toward the city. After passing the station wagon, they came up behind a cruising motorcycle with a man at the bars and a girl on the back. The girl, in a tiny green bikini, seemed very comfortable, with her hands on her legs, not bothering to hold on to the man. Behind her whipped her long blond hair.

"If they hit a bump," said Margot, "or even a rock or a board and have to put that bike down, there's not going to be any skin left on that girl. She's ninety-nine percent naked. I'd put pants and a jacket on."

"Maybe they're drunk. ... Margie, what do you think we'll be like when were old?"

Watching the motorcycle. "I don't know. What's the difference?"

"Do you think we'll ever come to hate each other?"

She looked over at him. "We're going to be fine, don't worry about it. Besides, if we break up, your new Bonnie ass Henney will take you in."

"Don't say that."

"She was all over you, at least with her eyes."

"That's a lie, and you know it. She was all over *you*, couldn't you see it? She did everything but ask you to take your clothes off so she could see more of your muscles."

With a laugh, "If you go there alone, she'll rape you."

"You're nuts, you're absolutely nuts—or pretending. I was thinking that if you were to deliver paintings for me, she'd grab you on the spot, send Tricia out to lunch, and drag you into the back room."

"Drag? Me? Uh—probably not."

But lifting a hand from the wheel and reaching for a stick of gum, he thought about the woman— her full, sensuous lips, her pretty eyes and face. He wondered what he would do if he were indeed somehow attacked by the woman. When his high beams suddenly came on, brightening the girl's back and her streaming hair, he tapped the floor switch to force the low beams on again. "Goddamn machines," he muttered. "Autronic Eye, my ass. They sell you a gadget, at a hefty price, of course, and it turns out to be more annoying than useful. And they take the money and invent more stupid things. It's mostly men that do that, right."

"I would think."

"Why does life have to be so full of bullshit?" he went on. "You can spend every day listening to people—the radio, the television, the newspaper, it doesn't matter—but all you hear from them is bullshit. And everything you buy is just a marketed bundle of bullshit."

"Come on, Shelly, take it easy. Think of something nice. Look at that girl's ass and her flying hair. Isn't that beautiful? Come on, no more cynicism."

"That is a pretty bottom, I'll admit."

"Or think of getting the one-man show and maybe becoming famous. Nice, right?"

But suddenly the dashboard sensor popped the high beams on again, lighting up the girl's back. The man driving the motorcycle showed his irritation at again seeing their intensified light in his mirrors by shoving his left hand out and giving them the finger. The girl, also annoyed, lifted the bikini top over her head, pulled it free of her hair, then let it go.

As the tiny green garment hit the Olds, then caught on the antenna, Shelly reached up and switched off the Autronic Eye. "Well, I guess they've said it all. They don't like my brights."

"They've both been pretty articulate. Let's pass them, I want to see her tits."

Pushing the accelerator down, he sent the Olds out into the passing lane. "Here we go," he said. "Do a quick sketch."

But when they had pulled alongside the motor-cycle, both riders gave them the finger. Then, weirdly, just as Margot caught her breath at the girl's breasts, the guy swerved them over close to the Olds and the girl reached out and snatched back her bikini top from the antenna. Then Shelly pushed the accelerator to the mat and sent them speeding away from the motorcycle.

CHAPTER 20

It was exactly one month later that Shelly turned left after the bridge, then slowed the Olds along the quiet, affluent street. The house, which they had not seen before, located in the tranquil suburb of Woodmere, near Avondale, was lit up completely by exterior lights. Numerous cars, obviously expensive, already lined the property.

"It's only seven," he said, glancing at the dash, then looking for a place to park. "We're not late, are we?"

"Park here. This is perfect."

After carefully backing in and shutting off, he puffed his cheeks, then exhaled. "Do you see that?" he said, his eyes large. "I've parked behind a Lincoln Continental. It's huge. It's gleaming. It's worth about a million dollars."

"Not quite, sweetheart, but it did take a pile to buy it. Bet you're glad you didn't dent it. But aren't you proud we've been invited? I'm telling you— you'd better keep painting, girl."

"Don't call me girl tonight, Margie, please."

"Sure. Don't worry."

"I can't believe it," he groaned. "All ten—they sold all ten pieces. I just can't believe it."

"Well, you'd better close your mouth, or you'll look funny walking into that mansion. So, Mr. S. Byrne—take a deep breath, okay?"

Indeed taking the breath, "Oh, and I'm glad you're here. I love you, Margie."

"I'm not going to respond to that. Just get out of the car."

The house, or mansion, as Margot had insisted it was, located on the St. Johns River, had obviously been designed, decorated and maintained to take the visitor's breath away. By actual size it was perhaps merely a large house, but by appearance it was truly a mansion. Its tall white pillars, of course lit at night, presented only a stately image. Just behind the house was a swimming pool, lit at night by underwater lights and surrounded by pretty tables and chairs under colorful umbrellas. To one side there was a long string of chaise lounges, each with a little martini table of its own. The manicured grounds, attended by a gardener, reached to the river. At the end of a dock a tidy boathouse, topped with a flag, protected a powerful lapstrake speedboat.

"Jesus Christmas!" uttered Margot, eyeing the long line of expensive and exotic cars of guests that had found space in the driveway. "Get a look at that, sweetheart. I wonder who owns the Corvette. Sweet as sugar, right? And with all the foreign machines here, I wouldn't be surprised if Enzo Ferrari himself shows up at this party."

"We're supposed to just go in," he said as they came to the front entrance. "So, how do I look?"

"You're actually going to ask me that? Look at them through the glass, the party's underway. If you're not going to pull the door open, I will, Miss Byrne."

"Stop calling me that, I mean it. Don't say it in there, Margie."

"You look fine—very modest, very classy. They will love the hair. ... Or maybe not. But it's gorgeous, I promise."

With a stern look, "So, I look okay?"

You could use a little lipstick, but yeah, you're fine. Stop worrying. You look very New York, very classy. And your hair—Jesus! Slay me now!"

He closed his eyes. "Okay, fine. Let's go in."

"So, pull the door open."

Obeying, he gave the long brass handle a turn, then pulled. They stepped inside to a foyer, where two men stood engaged in conversation, each with an empty martini glass in hand. Immediately they turned and smiled, and one of them pointed toward the hallway. Oddly at the middle of the foyer rested a professionally printed sign that requested all smoking to be taken outside due to insurance requirements for the hanging art. The foyer led directly into a long hallway lined with art of obvious quality and value, including drawings by both Picasso and Modigliani.

Off the hallway was a large open room well filled with people either engaged in conversation or moving about. Everything was bathed in white light, as if to present a pristine atmosphere. Beside a small table a woman was mixing drinks, and at the corner of the room a string quartet was playing classical pieces.

"Come on," said Margot in a low voice, "let's just walk around." And taking his hand, she led the way. "I smell alcohol."

But when they were halfway to the table Bonnie turned from a group conversation and gave them each a cordial hug. It was the first time they had seen her with her hair down. Curving down in such a way as to accentuate the gray eyes, the dark hair, as if swathed by an artist's brush, made its way to somewhere beyond, the shoulders. The black top, as if cut by a Renaissance sculptor, took the small breasts and made fruit of them. The gray slacks, again exquisitely cut, offered the rest of her like a Venus. The shoes, like diamond sandals on an angel, nearly forced the eyes away for the brightness of their sparkle. But the real killer of the image was the set of jewels at the neck.

"Oh, we're having a splendid time," she chortled. "Don't you like parties? I'm so very glad you're here. Now go over and get yourselves a drink, and I'll introduce you to some people." And lowering her voice, "Just smile, be sweet, and remember—there are a lot of collectors here. Oh, and if you would like something special to eat, just go back to the kitchen and tell my chef I sent you." And giving them a gentle push, she turned back to the group.

Later, as they walked by a window and looked out toward the water, Shelly, half the gin in his glass gone, remarked, "Boy, she's got class. What in God's name was that perfume? Did you smell it? Probably Parisian. Unbelievable!"

"Oh, I smelled something, all right," Margot returned, finishing the gin in her glass. "But it was more like pussy than perfume."

"Hey, be nice. This is a nice party."

"I'm just reading the words scribbled on the restroom wall of my mind. The woman's a walking twat."

Giving the gin a swirl, "Let's sit."

After taking to a loveseat that seemed to afford a good view of the room, Margot said, "I suppose we'd better not spill our drinks."

"Really? Because I was thinking that if I did, she would just order a new loveseat."

Leaning closer, "She wouldn't do it, Shelly, she would have it done. She seems a little blank about the dollar count. Somebody's doing it for her."

For some reason they both looked across the room at Tricia, who stood smart and sexy, along with Henney, talking to the same group of rich-looking older people. Tricia's hair, especially alluring, glowed as if it had been polished. Her lips, glossed as if by an artist using a sable brush, seemed molten. Her face was bright, her smile sensuous. Her glasses were gone, held at the ready in her free hand. Her martini was like a ghost in her other hand. And the dress, a white something or other that displayed elegantly the tops of her breasts, was a sensual dream.

Cocking his head, Shelly queried, "Do you think Tricia's doing it?"

With a sigh, "Sounds plausible. Unless it's some financial advisor or a lawyer. But Tricia's smart enough to handle probably all of Bonnie's finances—both personal and for the gallery."

"Well, looking at this place, I'm guessing that's one hell of a lot of money."

Margot nodded. "I'll bet Bonnie doesn't even know how much money she's got. Would you like to bet?"

Taking a sip from his glass, "Nope."

Leaning especially close and dropping her voice further, "Personally, I don't think Bonnie has any underwear on."

He tipped the glass, finished the drink, then gave the ice a clinky shake. "Thanks, Margie, I needed that image in my brain. Thanks a lot."

"I'm telling you, Shelly, there's so much money in this room you can smell it. And it ain't the odd man out either—nearly everybody here is rich."

"Granted. But I know poverty when I see it, too. Obviously there are a number of artists here. The guy with the long hair, standing by the piano—I picked up turpentine on him, I swear to God."

With a shrug, "At least he's got a dinner jacket on."

"Probably the only one he owns."

She gave a low snoggy sound and pushed her bangs aside. "I can tell you something else though. Our dear Bonnie Henney's one goddamn hell of a drinker. Seriously! I thought *I* was an alcoholic. I've been watching her. *That* is a really serious boozer. And have you noticed? She doesn't show it. For that kind of drinker—the stuff's like water."

With a sigh, "Let's go talk to some people. Come on, Margie, let's pick somebody out."

"This is odd for you."

"How about the guy with the long hair?"

With a shake of her head, "Don't call it long. That's not long. Yours—is long."

Oddly, as they left the loveseat the music from the quartet stopped, and the musicians laid their instruments down and began to saunter toward the liquor table. Then a woman slipped in at the piano and began quietly to play and then to sing beautifully a very poignant *Somewhere Over The Rainbow*. After the first line, the man with the long hair seemed a little to melt, simply leaning against the piano. But as Margot and Shelly approached he straightened himself up, produced a broad smile, and stuck out his hand.

"Hi," he said, his eyes going to Shelly's hair, "I'm Roger Happert."

For a moment Shelly merely looked at the hand. But then he shook it and returned, "Shelly Byrne. This is Margot Bernard."

"Oh, the painter, yeah," said Happert, his eyes still on the hair and as if Margot had not been introduced. "Nice hair—I really like it. Hey, I've heard about you. Your stuff's heating things up at the gallery. Good for you. I'm in the gallery, too."

"Yes, I remember seeing your name on a yellow piece. Yellow squares?"

Trying yet failing to get a hand through his thick hair, which came only a little below his ears, "Yeah, that's me. That's what I do, all squares. It's great, I love it. I haven't seen your work. What's it like?"

"Mostly spatial right now, and mostly in pastel colors. But a few are dark."

"Yeah, wow. But Bonnie really says you're great. So, neat!" And offering his hand now to Margot, "And you're a writer? Hi."

But, loathe to shake the hand, she merely turned and scanned the crowd.

Withdrawing his hand, he took in the face, the hair, the muscular body. He had never liked physically strong women. But then he looked up and said, "Hey, here comes Bonnie. Watch your asses, people."

"And now, please," said Henney, taking Shelly's arm, then Margot's, "I'd like you two to come with me."

As they walked Shelly leaned into Henney, but could detect only the perfume he had smelled earlier, mixed of course with alcohol. But the touch of their bodies seemed a little electric, especially when the singer began to sing, 'Smile though your heart is breaking. . . .'

She led them to the small group she had been entertaining before. "I want to introduce to you all," she said, "the artist Shelly Byrne and the author Margot Bernard. Margot is published and I'm going to offer Shelly—right now—his first one-man show with the gallery. And that show, if he accepts, will be hung toward the end of September. . . . Shelly, how about it?"

Later, as they headed home along Riverside Avenue, Shelly, who had decided he felt too tipsy to drive, lowered his window for fresh air and said, "I'm not used to that kind of thing. That was intensely social. I mean, as a social situation."

"But you're the one," returned Margot, "who suggested we go talk to people."

Ignoring this, "My dad and mom had those things all the time, but I never took part. It was usually just a bunch of drunk women with their sweaty tits hanging out. This, however, was nice, I have to admit. Very tastefully done."

"You'll get over it. You were very nice—and pretty."

"Thank you. But I felt like I was being defined somehow, especially when she offered me the show."

"Oh, come on, Shelly. Please!"

"When we stood there with her and Tricia and that group of old people, and she suddenly offered me the show, I instantly felt like I should decline. Sorry."

"No, that's okay. I'm just glad you didn't follow your impulse. I won't say it would have been insulting for you to do that—insulting to Bonnie, to Tricia, to the guests, to me, to yourself, to all you've wanted and worked for, to practically the whole goddamn world. No, I won't say that."

"Look, Margie, it's just you and me here, okay? Of course I wouldn't have actually done that. I'm just saying I got a warning of some kind, from within."

"Yeah, well, I don't really want to hear about it. She offered you the show, and you accepted and thanked her. So, just go with it and forget, if you can, all the sensitivity stuff. Oh, and not a group show, but a one-man show, your first one-man show. I mean, Jesus! Anybody can see she's taking a fucking chance on you. She's doing the mailings, the advertising, the better framing. And that guy with the dirty hair, what was his name?"

"Roger Happert."

"Yeah, well, I'm sorry, but the good man Roger, as anybody could see tonight, would have sucked everybody's dick in the room to get a one-man show. He even said he'd only been in group shows. But you got the show. Which means, she has confidence in you and your work, asshole."

He let his eyes go shut. "I know."

"So, then," she continued, with some incredulity, "don't be an asshole." And wheeling the Olds into the driveway and up to the garage and shutting down, "Look, I don't want to talk about it anymore. You need to go in and—sorry, *we* need to go in and pull out everything you have that even resembles the paintings she sold. Then we should look at your supplies and get what you need. Then you need to fix your mind on painting. Agreed, Miss S. Byrne?"

Sighing, "Yes."

And lifting a forefinger, "And one more thing. I've known people who have done what you just about did back there. When they're offered the very thing they've been striving for, they turn away from it, like they had the guts to want it, but not the guts to possess it. I hate people like that. Have the courage to possess what you want. Now, I will love you, and I will screw you, but by goodness I will not stick fucking boards under you and prop you up. If you're too goddamn chicken to possess what you want, then I know I can't trust you to possess me."

"And if it destroys me or my art?"

"Failing at this or succeeding at this will not hurt either you or your art. But running away from it will destroy both. Now, I don't care if you have to drink your way through this thing, you're going to do it. Okay?" And when there was no response, "Hey! You have to say okay or not okay. Now I'm listening, and I want to hear it—one or the other. Say it!"

"Okay."

When all the guests had left, and even the party crew, housekeeper, and chef had gone, Henney went to the downstairs bar, opened its doors, and made herself a margarita. This in hand, she climbed the staircase to go up to her bedroom. Halfway up, she stopped, turned toward the old clock, and noted the time. She could easily have simply thrown the big white face a glance and not broken her step. But sometimes, such as after successful parties, she often had an inclination to be more elaborate in her noting the time, as if to make a more definite point to refer to in the future.

At the landing she noted that there was no light from Tricia's door at the end of the hall. In her room she set the drink on the night table, pulled the covers back, and got into bed. Why did she love to go to bed this way, with all her clothes on, even down to the black strap heels? Only God, she reasoned, could say. But as she would not bother him with anything so mundane, she had long before resolved never to know.

After another draw from the margarita, she went to the table, retrieved her business address book, and brought it to bed. Opening it to the A's, she began to make a mental tally of those who might be interested in coming to the show.

Twenty minutes later, the margarita gone, she set the book aside, got up and went into the bathroom. On her way back to bed, she took the top off, then the slacks, dropped them into the clothes bin, and stood naked before the tall mirror beside the dresser. She had never liked underwear and was glad she had not felt compelled to wear any for the party. For a moment she looked at her image, letting her eyes move slowly up and down. But then she turned away, went to the night table, took out the .38, and slid it under the pillow.

After slipping into bed and switching off the light, she pulled the covers up to her chin and lay in the darkness. Yes, it had been a successful evening. As a breeze from the river moved up the back lawn, through the curtains, and into the room she thought of Margot's brown eyes and strong arms, of Shelly's green eyes and beautiful hair. They had both smelled so fresh and clean. She was glad she had not picked up from them some awful perfume scent, which she might find difficult to forget.

CHAPTER 21

September

When the doorbell chimed Margot left the kitchen. Through the door's little window she could see the smiling faces of Henney and Tricia. After ushering them inside, she threw an appreciative glance at the gleaming, silver Maserati, then closed the door.

"I am so glad to get here for a visit," said Henney as both she and Tricia removed their scarves and smoothed their hair. "And Riverside is such a charming area. I just love it around here."

Margot chuckled. "We're actually not far from you. Just across the inlet."

"Yes, yes," returned Henney, with a wave. "Well, you'll have to swim over and knock on our back door sometime."

For some reason the use of the plural pronoun made Margot look at Tricia—at the blond hair, the glasses, the expensive light sweater and slacks, even the rich sandals and lipstick-colored toenails.

Forcing her gaze back to Henney, she took in the sweater and pants and shoes, the value of which only God himself knew.

Now feeling quite poor, Margot led them to the piano room, where things for tea had been laid. The windows were up, and there was a breeze coming in from the side yard. As they all took a seat, suddenly she felt she must apologize for the shabby furniture, although she had no intention of telling them about the money from Shelly's dad. "Sorry for the crummy chairs," she offered. "We're a little loose here. Hope you don't mind. You might see a mouse or two run by."

Henney threw another wave. "Oh, Margot, this is nice, charming, a real artist's house. Very nice. I think I smell turpentine. And do you have a writing studio?"

"I do. It actually smells a little of turpentine, too, as I'm not far from Shelly. Sometimes I have to close the door."

When Shelly came in they took tea and cookies and chatted about the weather and how it was nice to live close to a river. After the breeze died, Margot offered to bring a fan, but no one seemed to think it was necessary.

"That's a very nice car," offered Margot at length. "It's a Maserati, isn't it?"

"It is," returned Henney, with a flashy smile. "It's very powerful, very fast, and quite glamorous. Tricia calls it the Mas-erotic. We sometimes take it out on the highway and let it run."

Again she caught the *we*. "And when it gets to run, how fast does it go?"

Giving a delicate scratch to the side of her nose, "I'm not really sure, but it seems to be quite content at a hundred and fifty."

"It will go faster," offered Tricia, giving the inside of her leg a scratch, as if in parallel with Henney's scratch to the nose, "but Florida highways, as Bonnie says, seem to be a little short on pavement."

Margot could not refrain from following Tricia's lips as she spoke. She pictured her driving her own car, perhaps a Jaguar, with the top down, of course, and then getting out near a sunny beach and walking near the water in not much more than would be legal even on a French beach.

Later, when they had taken drinks to the living room to look at paintings, Margot stood aside with Tricia while Shelly and Henney pulled older canvases from their propped stacks and set them out in the light.

"So, Tricia," she said, standing close, "what kind of car do you drive?"

Tricia adjusted the napkin around her glass of iced gin. "I have a little Corvette. It's blue and white."

"Was that the one I saw at the party?"

"It was the only one there, I think."

"That is a beautiful car."

"I love it," cooed Tricia. "It's not that fast, but it's so pretty. When I first saw it, I just couldn't resist. I just have to have it, I said—it *has* to be mine."

Margot looked as closely as she could at the China-blue eyes behind the thick glasses. "What's its top speed?"

"Mine tops out at about a hundred and ten. It only has a 283 in it. Zero to sixty is about eight. It'll do the quarter in about sixteen. No, it's not fast."

"But it's sexy."

"Exactly. And very nice around town. I get lots of comments. From the things people have said to me, I imagine about half the moms out there would love to own one. It's interior is quite pretty. Maybe a little cheap, but pleasantly intimate. There's not a lot of room to move around, so I'm not going to get pregnant in it, let's put it that way."

Margot did not know what it was exactly that made this woman so erotically attractive to her, but statements like this certainly contributed to the allure. For a moment she said nothing, but then simply, "Right. Well, there you are."

After licking gin from the rim of her glass, Tricia smiled, then queried, "And do you like your car?"

Actually now leaning away from her a little, "Yes, it's nice. It's big, comfortable, lots of space— enough for hauling paintings and groceries and, I guess, yes, for getting pregnant in, if that's what one wished to do."

"So," said Henney, raising her voice a little after swallowing a mouthful of gin, "all these are finished?"

Shelly nodded. "Signed and cataloged."

"Do you keep a photographic record of them?"

"No."

"Hmm. Well, I like what I see. Some of the abstracts are terribly soft, like a Corot sky. And yet some seem to move to the rough pastels of a

Boudin sky. You're pretty convincing in both directions actually. And the dark ones—very nice."

He took a sip of his gin, as if to appreciate this. "But, you can see there are numerous styles and motifs. I guess most of them wouldn't go well together in a show."

She gave a quick shrug. "Probably not. But—" Here she paused, noticing her glass was empty. "Might I have a refresher? I don't want to trouble you."

Quickly Margot snatched the glass and left. A minute later she returned, handed the glass to Henney, saying that she had also added more ice, then took up her place by Tricia.

"So, Bonnie," said Shelly, "what were you saying about my mixed styles?"

"Well, I was about to say—before I became thirsty—that they can be shown together, within reason, of course. The limitation seems usually to be the simple limitations of collectors. Some of them, you know, are quite stup—" Here she was stopped by a serious scowl from Tricia. "Well," she continued, "for many collectors, inconsistency in an artist's work indicates a lack of direction and conviction, of maturity of ideas. When they encounter inconsistency in style they usually say the artist was experimenting. Which, of course, is ridiculous. Van Gogh, Picasso, and many others have shown no real consistency in their work at all." Bringing the glass to her nose, she inhaled the vapors, then put it to her heavily lipsticked lips and simply drank half its contents.

As if mesmerized, the others watched her. The glass, well marked with ruby-red prints of her bottom lip, seemed to float like some crystalline butterfly as she fairly gloried over the paintings. It was as if they were all counting the seconds until the glass would again be empty and the next request made to refill it.

"I'm seeing," said Henney, "a very pleasant inconsistency in your things, one that I look for because it usually tells me whether the artist is telling the truth or not. Frankly, the first thing that tells me an artist is lying is consistency in the work. Of course, it looks the same because he's found himself. Sure he has—like hell he has! I've got a message for them. If they ever really find themselves, they'll see they're just a crock of shit like everybody else is. But they all want to make it look like they've found themselves and there's no shit there. But invariably amateurs try to make all their work look the same. They even get rid of the work that doesn't look the same. They're terribly pathetic. I'm looking for genuine artists who are genuine people. Artists are people, and people are not consistent. I don't want to see something artificial, I want to see something real."

"Do you think my stuff's real?"

"Sure. Otherwise, I wouldn't be here. It isn't a qualitative thing, though. To actually *be* real, to achieve reality, is impossible, if you think about it. So, it's a matter of being more or less real, it's a quantitative thing. It's simply lying less and telling the truth more."

"But you initially asked for the same style."

"Of course. That's what I'm saying. That's pretty much all the collectors can usually handle. Some of them are smart, logical, and know art, but most are just interested in making a good investment. And that means they want a painting they've paid a lot of money for to look like it came from a certain artist." Then, with a shrug, "These linear things are quite good. But this show has to be all spatial things, just like the ones we sold. And with mostly pastel colors too. But if the show's successful, then later we can include the linears and some other things you've done."

With a tone of impatience, Tricia said, "It's all pretty logical, Shelly. We have to be careful."

Henney lowered her glass and looked at Shelly, then at Margot. "And you understand why, don't you? Because we're raising the prices for your work."

Shelly looked at Margot, then at Tricia, then at Henney. "By how much?"

Tricia cleared her throat. "By ten times."

"So," said Margot, her eyes growing larger, "the 24-by-30's will be priced at $4,000, and the 28-by-36's at $6,000?"

Tricia pushed her glasses up. "Correct."

"Yeah," said Henney, looking into her glass, "Tricia's pretty smart, and that's what she advises, so we're going to go with it." She gave what was left in the glass a swirl. "And besides, I've looked at your work, and I know it's really, really good. I believe in you, okay? So, don't worry about the show, it's going to be fine. Just get to work."

Margot set her glass down. "And, just so we're clear," she said, looking at Henney, then at Tricia, "we're talking legitimate here, right?"

Henney smiled. "Of course. That's all I ever talk, frankly. Since Pollock died collectors have started seriously to buy modern art. It's as simple as that. Of course, if I'm wrong about your work, then I'm wrong, and it will never be worth that much. But I'm pretty sure I'm not wrong."

For some reason, everyone looked at Tricia. The woman simply blinked and said, "Maybe you haven't been aware of it, but you're sitting on a gold mine here."

"So," said Shelly, turning to Henney, "how much is all of this worth exactly?"

After a slight shrug, "I have no idea. Tricia has a head for things like that, but I don't. I just know the art."

Margot took a step away from Tricia. "Tricia, what would you say its worth?"

A wrinkle on her forehead, Tricia took a sip of her drink. "It can't be calculated right now, any more than it could have before the show. Everything in every market is always in flux—it's a law, like gravity. Any figure I could give could be so far off the mark as to be useless, even misleading, especially since Shelly is young and still producing. The art market itself is unbelievably complex. Critics look, then put a thumb up or down. Unfortunately what they say has an effect on collectors and the market as a whole. Collectors look to the critics for guidance, so they won't make a stupid investment, which is not actually uncommonly done. So, I'm sorry, but I wouldn't even hazard a guess. Let's just say, Bonnie knows her art, and I know my money, so I think you're in good hands."

Henney looked into her glass, then at Margot. "You apologized for your chairs," she said.

"They're fine. But we are concerned about your leaky roof." Then she held the glass out again for Margot to take.

"Shall I get you another?"

With a smile, "No. We have to go. . . . So, we've framed your new things, and they look really nice. The other moldings were, well, somewhat rustic compare to these. I think you'll be pleased. . . . Tricia, ready? We'll see you both at the show. It was nice visiting."

As they heard the Maserati pull away Shelly gave Margot a nudge and said, "This is pretty neat, right?"

"Uh-huh."

"My dad's money, your book, the paintings."

"Uh-huh. But don't ask me why it's happening. I've never really had a good relationship with the word *why.* Oh, and we'd better buy more gin. She drank about two thirds of the bottle."

CHAPTER 22

The gallery façade seemed especially well lit as they approached. In the middle of the sidewalk, a few feet from the entrance stood a classy A-frame sign announcing the opening of the one-man show of the artist S. Byrne. In the big front window hung two of Shelly's 28-by-36 paintings.

Not far from the entrance Shelly halted to ask how he looked. He had worn black pants, a heavily starched and ironed white, long-sleeved cotton shirt, and had even shined his shoes. They had taken dinner at a nearby restaurant, just off the square, to celebrate the show. Unfortunately he had spilled a little wine on one leg of the pants.

"You can't see it?" he queried earnestly.

Margot bent down to look. "You know," she said impishly, "we could get arrested for this. . . . No, I can't see it. The entire spot is gone. It was just a little red wine on black material, so forget it."

"Are you positive? And you don't see anything on my shirt? Not a single spot?"

"No, Shelly, I told you, there's nothing. You goofy queers are all so fastidious! Come on, let's go in."

But after looking up at his two paintings in the window, he said, "I'm getting nervous. I think I'm going to be sick, Margot."

The other blinked. When she got Margot instead of Margie, she knew something was up. "Really? Can you make it into the bathroom? . . . Okay, okay, take a deep breath. Good. And again, and again, and again. Good, very good. Okay, you cannot throw up here, you just cannot do it."

He gave his head a couple of vigorous shakes. "I'm really not well."

She put a hand on his arm. "Okay, listen. . . . Your paintings are mediocre, they're bad, and actually about half of them are just pure shit. And nobody in the whole goddamn universe is going to buy anything tonight, unless they're paid to do it. I personally wouldn't buy a single fucking one of them. And that is the fucking truth. So, if you go and puke from worrying about your mediocre art, you're an absolute dipshit."

"That's Southern talk."

"I know, moron. You don't deserve any better. So, just take another breath and calm down."

He stopped taking the deep breaths and looked at her. "You know, Margie, I think that helped."

"I'm not going to stand here and give you a lecture. They're just paintings, Shelly, and you're actually not the greatest goddamn artist in the world."

Swallowing, "Uh—I think I feel better. I think I'm going to be all right. Great! Thank you. All right, let's go in."

"So," she said, herself halting, "how do you think I look?"

"You?" And taking a quick look, "You're fine. I love the jeans. Come on."

Tricia greeted them at the door. She had left the glasses close by, on the desk. The effect was the same as at the party—stunning to the point of being erotic. The blond hair, blue eyes, and milk-white skin made Margot catch her breath. And at Tricia's neck was a string of genuine pearls that were obviously meant to lead the beholder's eyes down to her cleavage.

"Bonnie's in the back," she cooed, with a quick lick of her rubied lips. "We've had a few people in already, but the big crowd should be showing up in about twenty minutes."

As they left her, Margot whispered, "Was she real? Talk about beautiful!"

"I know. But Bonnie said she's just about blind without the glasses."

Both sides of the gallery were lined with exquisitely framed work. On a pedestal table at center gallery were glossy catalogs with Shelly's picture, artist's statement, and short biography.

"I think S. Byrne is already famous," offered Henney, coming from the back room. "I just sold the blue one. Come on, Shelly, you can have the honor of marking it as sold."

At mid-gallery he pressed the sticker onto the painting's description tag for them all to see, then took a step back to appreciate the picture.

"Don't tell me," said Tricia to Henney, "it was the gray-haired man."

"Yep," returned the other simply. "He got home, decided to buy, and called me just now."

Later, when Margot had shut the engine off in the driveway, she said, "You know why she had you put that sold sticker on, don't you?"

"So she wouldn't have to set her glass down."

"Correct. She's terribly glamorous, isn't she? With the Maserati and the mansion—what a woman! But I still can't get over Tricia. God!"

"I know, right?"

Margot looked over at him. Even in the dark the hair seemed to glow. "So, when is it going to sink in? You just sold out your first one-man show on the first night."

Momentarily, "And what does that mean?"

"Well, you can't tell me Bonnie isn't already planning another show. And our phone's probably going to start ringing, I'm sorry."

"We don't need the money, Margie. With my dad's money, we're actually pretty rich."

"Your dad's money just means you can paint without pressure, and your stuff can be—"

"Pure?"

"Yes. Reasonably."

After a deep breath, "Margie, I am not a pure person."

"Neither am I. That's why I added the qualifier, dear."

"And as for the pressure? I've never felt so much pressure in my life."

"But it's a good pressure. So, get over it, please. . . . Come on, let's go in, Mr. S. Byrne. I want to take you to bed and get your autograph."

The trees around the house, especially the sycamores, had provided a golden, greenish brown carpet for the trick-or-treaters to shuffle over. Shelly watched from a window as a princess, a hobo, a vampire, a witch, and a boy in a sport coat, not bothering to take the sidewalk, crossed the yard to get to the front door. He himself would have done the same, he thought. When the doorbell chimed he opened the door and looked at the collection of characters.

"Trick-or-treat!" they yelled as the door was opened.

"And what do we have?" he asked, grasping the bag of treats. "A bunch of television actors, I think, or maybe some characters out of a book."

A little girl, about ten years old and in a white dress, raised her hand, as if asking permission to speak, then replied that she was a princess. Then a boy about the same age, in a black cape and with big scary teeth, announced that he was Dracula. After him, the boy in the sport coat, seemingly also of elementary school age, stepped forward. Grinning, he pulled a gun from his pants pocket, and with his finger on the trigger shoved it up into Shelly's face, and shouted out that he was Al Capone.

Shelly caught his breath as he stared at the weapon. Instantly he recognize it as a real snub-nosed revolver. Worse, he could see, even in the dim porch light, bullet noses in the cylinder.

Swallowing hard, he moved his eyes from the gun to meet the boy's sparkling eyes.

"All right," he said to everyone cheerily, but with his heart pounding, "so, you're all very scary. I give up." And reaching into the bag of candy, "Hold your bags up and I'll give you each two big candy bars."

In unison they gave a raucous shout of approval, then took turns holding out their bags. As they walked away, he said, "Hey, Mr. Capone, come here. You're a gangster, huh? Very nice costume, did your mom make it?"

"Nah, I did. It's just a coat. I didn't have a hat."

"And that's a nifty gun you've got there. Can I see it?" When happily he handed it over Shelly pushed the latch and swung the cylinder out. "Is this your gun?"

"No, ma'am. It's my dad's. He said I could take it."

"Do you have any more bullets, or is this it?"

"That's all, ma'am. I was supposed to take them out, but I forgot."

Tipping the gun, Shelly ejected the cartridges into his hand, then closed the cylinder and handed the gun back. Noting the other kids were waiting at the corner, he said to the boy, "Listen, you've got a great costume. But you could've really hurt somebody with this gun. When you take it home tonight, tell your dad he can come get the ammunition from me, if he wants it. You tell him where I live. I just don't want you having it when you're out having fun. Okay?"

"All right, ma'am. Thank you for the candy bars. Most people don't give us that much."

"Sure. You go on now, your scary friends are waiting. Oh—what's your name?"

"Danny."

"What's your last name, Danny."

"Lucci, ma'am."

A shiver went through him. "What's your dad's name, Danny?"

"Robert."

"Oh, that's nice. Do you have an uncle?"

"Yeah. Uncle Joey. He's at home now. He lives with us. . . . Got to go, ma'am."

Suddenly Shelly became aware that his mouth was open and that his heart was pounding again. Then he called as the boy walked away, "What's your uncle do, Danny? Does he work?"

"No, ma'am. He just sits around with my dad drinkin' beer. Sometimes he mows the yard. Gotta go!"

After watching the group move up King Street, Shelly went inside, locked the door, and turned off the outside light for the evening.

"Guess who just came to the door with a loaded gun?"

Margot looked up from the typewriter. "Uh-oh."

"I actually want you to guess."

"I don't do well with this kind of thing, as you know."

"You're not going to do well with this one either, I'm afraid."

"Who?"

Shelly rolled his eyes. "No, no. You have to guess."

Margot pushed her chair back and stood. "Okay, stop the game. A loaded gun is serious. Tell me right now who it was."

"Your nephew-in-law—I guess that's what he is."

"Danny?"

"Correct."

"He lives around here?"

"So," he continued, "they yell their trick-or-treat stuff, like any bunch of regular kids. Then a couple of them tell me what their costumes are supposed to be. Finally he steps up—and of course I didn't know him from anybody, and wouldn't have if I hadn't asked his name. He pulls a .38, just like ours, sticks it in my face, and announces he's Al Capone. His finger is on the trigger, and I can see bullets in the cylinder."

Incredulous, she sat down again. "Good God! What did you do?"

"Well, I just about died from heart failure, I can tell you that. My heart was pounding like crazy. I mean, I thought the kid was going to pull the fucking trigger. Jesus! Margie, the thing was loaded, and the muzzle was in my face, and his finger was right there on the trigger, ready to pull it."

"I asked you already—what did you do?"

"What should I have done, shoot the little bastard? I just tried to be calm and gave them their goddamn treats. I even doubled it."

"You gave them two of those candy bars—each?"

"I did. Then, when they were leaving, I called him back and asked to see his gun. He seemed like a nice kid. He just handed it to me, so I took the bullets out, and gave it back to him. He said he was supposed to unload it, but forgot. Then I asked his name and—when I heard Lucci I asked if he had an uncle. So, guess where your ex-husband is living? With them."

"You know," she said, "Joey's not really stupid. He's not smart, but no, he's not at all stupid. He's here for a reason. And I'll bet you anything it's because I signed the papers saying I didn't need the alimony anymore. He's going to ask me for money, I know it. . . . But Danny didn't know who you were?"

"No, but when I took the bullets I told him to tell his dad he could come get them if he wanted them back. So, he might show up."

"Yeah, that would be Bobby. But my guess is—Joey will be the one showing up." And pressing her back against the chair, "Okay, okay. This is not a coincidence. I will bet anything that Joey will show up at this house. Goddammit!"

CHAPTER 23

Two days later Shelly opened the door and stood looking down at Joey Lucci. A shiver went through him as he took in the grin, the menacing eyes, the whole demeanor he had picked up from Margot's description and from the photo he had seen of him in police uniform.

"Hi, I'm Joey," he said, continuing to grin, his eyes on the long hair. "Is Margot around?"

For a single, ugly moment Shelly pictured Margot having sex with the man, but then switched the image off and said, "Yeah. I'll get her?"

"Can I come in?"

Reaching for the inner door to close it, "No, just wait there. I'll get her."

Moments later Margot, carrying a paper lunch bag, opened the door and looked down at him through the screen. "Hi," she said simply.

"Yeah, hi," he returned, with a chuckle. "How's things goin'?"

"What do you want?"

The grin disappeared. "Yeah, well, I came to get the ammo back. That's what your whatever said to do, right?"

Pushing the screen door open, she handed him the bag, then pulled the door closed again. She watched as he dumped the cartridges into his hand, dropped one, picked it up, then shoved them into his jeans pocket. As he wadded up the bag and began to grin at her again, she wondered how in God's name she could ever have been intimate with him. When he held the bag out, she opened the door, took it, and pulled the door shut again. Which was odd, she thought, since she had the distinct, powerful feeling of not being afraid of him.

"Hey," he said, "can I come in?"

"Why?"

"Just to talk. Old times."

"No."

"Hey, you look good. You been liftin'?"

"Some."

With a chuckle, "Hey, me too." Here he made a fist and pulled it to his chin, tightening his bicep. But the muscle did not show through the jacket, so he lowered the arm, gave a little shrug, and asked again if he could come in.

"No."

With another shrug, "Okay. ... Hey, listen, I want to borrow some money."

"No."

"I need two thousand, and that's all. I apologize for borrowing it, but I need it. And I'll pay it back, I give you my word, Margot. I know you've got it, or you wouldn't have signed off on the alimony thing. Oh, and I was at the art opening. I went early and then just left. But I saw the prices. You guys are raking it in. So, how about it? Just two thousand, and I'll walk away."

"No. Use your own money. You have a job, you're a policeman, remember?"

"I'm not one anymore. I turned in the badge, and all that."

"Yeah?"

"I was kind of suspended."

"What for?"

"I don't know, maybe I beat one too many guys up, girls too, I guess." And when she said nothing to this, but merely looked at him, he said, "I know what yous are, both of yous. Yous are two fucking lesbians, that's what."

"He's a man, Joey."

Momentarily, "Yeah—like my ass he is! He's a fag, that's what, and so are you. You're both queers. ... Now, if yous don't want the whole world to know that, then just loan me the money I need, that's all. Just loan it to me, and I'll be gone, that's all."

"No."

"Well, this is Florida—yous are really illegal, I don't know whether yous know that. Yous should check the laws. Besides, people don't like queers. Now, there's the new book, I know, and there's the painting thing goin', and you don't need the alimony anymore. So, yous need to share. Two thousand, and I walk away. What do you say?"

"No."

"Ah, come on, why not?"

"You're being naïve. Half the female writers out there are lesbians. And an artist? Really? You know your problem, Joey? You've never read a whole book in your life. You need to get an art history book and do some reading."

"Yous're homosexuals, for Christ's sake!"

"No, we're not, Joey. But, you know what? Maybe we are. So what? Half the writers and artists out there are weird, or they wouldn't be doing what they do, you dumb fuck. Writers, painters, dancers, singers, musicians, actors. You are so stupid, Joey—you're ignorant and stupid."

"It's illegal!" he shot back. "And it ain't popular."

"Yeah—like blackmail."

"It's Florida. They'll come after yous both. They'll burn your house down!"

Casually she took a step back, put a hand on the door and slowly pushed it shut.

Shelly was waiting for her in the kitchen. "How," he asked, shaking his head, "did you ever get mixed up with him?"

"I don't know."

"You don't know—yeah, you do. What was it, his crank?"

"Maybe. What's the difference?"

"He's scum, Margie, anybody can see it. You're brilliant, you must have seen it."

"Okay, so I saw it. So what?"

"Margie, you married him! You were actually his wife. And now he's coming after us. You told me he was a mean one and had shot a lot of people. Oh, and by the way, I think his muscles are bigger than yours. Be serious about this, okay?"

She looked at him. Taking in the anxiety on the face, the fear in the pretty green eyes, she replied simply, "Okay. But it might have to cook for awhile."

"But you'll do something?"

"Yes."

December

From her studio window Margot watched as a single pigeon, apparently straying from its usual hunting grounds at the hospital dumpster, carefully searched the environs of the neighbor's trash cans. For some reason, the bird seemed especially symbolic for her, as she had not been able to take her mind off their predicament caused by Joey. Why, she asked herself, did life have to be replete with predators and victims, when all most people seemed to need or want was to find their daily bread and enjoy a little prosperity?

Taking a sip of her tea, she turned from the window, returned to the typewriter, and looked down at the page. How was she to write this character of the person she loved into the story? And why did there have to be a story at all? New fiction was coming out all the time that had virtually no story line, no artificial and hence cumbersome plot to titillate the reader and sell the book. Just why did humans require a contrivance to get their attention? Why did they have to be so linear, so intentional, so competitive, so pragmatic? Why did so many of them, as evidenced by the moronic shows on television, and yes, even readers too, have such a song-and-dance, who-done-it, who-gets-the-girl mentality? Perhaps she too should just abandon the whole plot-contrivance approach to fiction. What a fucking crucible writing was!

She put the cup down, then grabbed her lifting gloves and left. Throwing the door to the exercise room open, she marched in, pulled on the gloves, tossed aside her sweatshirt, checked the weight level on the bar, and lay down on the bench. After adjusting her position for comfort, she gripped the bar, took three deep breaths, pushed until the bar was clear of the supports, lowered it to her chest, then drew another deep breath and held it as she pressed the weight three times. With the bar aloft, she exhaled, then lowered the bar to the brackets and got up. Three times she walked around the bench to give her heart rate time to return to normal. While doing this she nearly always recalled the words of a high school coach that the faster the heart rate returns to normal, the more in shape that heart is. Taking the position again on the bench, she repeated the exercise, this time doubling it, but taking a breath following the first three presses.

"Well," said Shelly coming in and taking a seat to watch, "I can smell the sweat in here. I suppose that means it's honest labor."

Getting up and beginning her walk around the bench, "No, it just means I need a shower. Isn't it weird that if you did something like this, and even wore the same shirt for a month, you wouldn't smell at all?"

With a shake of his head, "Well, forget the labor comment, you smell good to me, so keep it up."

"You like my smell?"

"I do," he answered, "as I've said probably a thousand times."

"I just like to hear it."

"So, let me watch some more, I like to see the hair under your arms."

"Don't be nasty," she returned, picking up the hand exercisers. "What're you doing in here smelling me, tired of sniffing turpentine?"

Momentarily, "I can't paint. What're you doing in here yourself?"

With a sigh and reaching for the dumbbells, "I can't write."

He wiped a finger on his jeans to get some paint off. He watched as she took a breath, held it, then lifted the dumbbells straight out to her side, then up over her head. He could see why people looked at her muscles. Finally he queried, "Why can't you write?"

Setting the weights down, "I don't know. Why can't you paint?"

"I don't know."

The next day, Margot got the key from the hook on the kitchen wall and went out to the garage. Removing the padlock, she stepped inside. In the spring she would move her weights out here.

Then she relocked the door and walked back to the house. As she had not worn a jacket or even a sweater, she began to shiver. Her eyes went to the palm tree across the street. How odd it seemed to have one of the most recognized symbols of the tropics growing there in the middle of winter. Grasping the cold handle of the screen door, she glanced at the street again, for a car was passing that had come from the hospital. Recognizing the driver, she hurried inside.

Giving a tap on the studio door, she pushed it open and leaned in. "Guess who I just saw driving past the house."

He did not look at her, but simply stuck the brush into the oil jar. "Just tell me."

Dropping into the overstuffed chair, she threw a leg over. "No, no. Guess. Since you like to make other people guess, now you guess."

With an impatient sigh, he ventured, "Your ex-husband."

"Nope. Guess again."

"No, Margie. You're breaking my concentration here. Now, who was it?"

"The man with the camera."

"Did he look like he was spying?"

"He seemed to be just driving by."

"Did he see you?"

Giving her bangs a push to the side, "I don't think so. But of course, this means he's around, he probably lives in the area. This is all we need, right?"

"Come on, Margie. Dad told us both that he had done it. When he died, it died with him. If the man lives around here, even somewhere else in the city, of course he's still here. But there's no reason to think he would still attempt to hurt us."

Annoyed, she raised a forefinger and said, "I think it's all cute, I really do. First we have the psycho dad after us, then the psycho killer, then the psycho photographer, then the psycho nephew, then the psycho ex. Have I left anybody out?"

He smiled. "How about my psycho mom. I'm sure she put a word or two into the mix. And how about the psycho librarian at the book-signing? But not much of that's realistic. Danny's not psycho. Maybe his father is, but not Danny, he's just a kid. I'm sure my dad couldn't have actually himself gotten the man out of prison. There must have been a significant entity that did it for him, even down to destroying the man's paperwork. And how about society and the culture, even the people at the beach, the way they looked at us?"

"So, you're saying what?"

"I'm saying it's an adversarial world, especially when it comes to the artist, the writer, the socially unacceptable. We have to be realistic about it all. Not everybody's a threat. We've had a lot of people on our side, like Tipper, the book store manager, Bonnie, Tricia."

She groaned. "Anything else, miss cool-headed-for-once?"

"Yes," he returned, "I am feeling cool-headed today. Which is fucking odd, isn't it? Anyway, all those entities saw us—and do see us—as being after them, too. The woman at the book-signing, for instance, clearly said you and your book were making an attack on the morals of society. And she's not alone there. People say the same about abstract art. And as far as our loving each other? Do we want to start counting the people who see us as my dad did, as being militantly against their families, their values, their society?"

"Your conclusion, miss philosophy?"

Now he directly met the brown eyes. "I identify two serious enemies here—my dad and your ex.

Tipper said we should keep an eye open for possible remnants of what my dad started. I would apply that to the man with the camera. But right now I think the only serious threat is Joey and maybe his brother."

She let her eyes go closed and her head fall back against the chair. At length she said, "Okay, I agree."

CHAPTER 24

Tricia looked up as they approached the bar, which was situated just off the pool but inside the house. Her hair fell over and around the glasses. Closing the black account book, she smiled, crossed her bare legs, and reached for her glass. The sexy and glamorous image could easily have given someone the idea that she was the owner of the property, instead of just the accountant.

"Shelly, Margot, hello," she offered, looking into her glass.

Margot's eyes went immediately to the lips, which had been painted a kind of Parisian hooker red. "Hi, Tricia," she returned, "what's happening?"

"Well, of all the four billion people in the world, I'm just one little piece of shit, like you two, and Bonnie, and J. Paul Getty. I feel like a piece of shit because our johnny-dick president did not call me this year to ask if he should tell Americans to build bomb shelters, or if he should invade Cuba, or if he should, just for fun, do a proxy war in Viet Nam."

"That's a smidgen negative. Nothing positive to say?"

"Sure. I got a few calls this year from nikki-dick Khrushchev, asking my opinion about whether he should send Yuri up or not, and whether he should divide Berlin, and whether he should test his hydrogen bomb, just to see if it worked. I told him each time to just go ahead, especially when he called about the bomb. Maybe, I told him, you'll get lucky and kill every living thing on the planet."

"So," said Shelly, "he listened to you, did he? Sounds like you have pull with the Kremlin. Maybe you're a Russian spy. Maybe you'll get caught and get the electric chair."

"I'm not waiting for them to catch me," she replied, "I'm going to sit right here and fry my liver and melt my brain. How are you two? Bonnie will be down in a minute." As they pulled out stools and sat she took in the comfortable clothes, the usual absence of makeup.

"Working on accounts?" queried Shelly.

"Of course. Always."

He groaned. "Ask me why I hate that kind of thing."

"Can I get you two something? How about a little something on ice?" And slipping from the stool, she opened the mirror-clad doors to expose the stock. "Is gin all right, or would you like something else? Stronger? Weaker? We have lots of scotch, all levels, except cheap, of course, and racks of excellent wines."

Margot let her eyes move over the myriad of bottles. "Gin's fine for me, Tricia."

"Yeah, me too," chimed Shelly, pretending he was not in awe. But then, "Do you actually keep track of all this?"

Somewhat unhappily, "Yes, I do."

"So," said Margot, "what do you think it is with alcohol, Tricia? What's the fascination we humans have for it, would you say?" And when there was a mere shrug as the other poured the drinks, "Does alcohol have some mystical call of the earth that attracts the sensitive person?" And with her eyes moving over the hips and down the legs, "Or would you say the real magic of alcohol comes simply from the enigmatic deficiencies of the sensitive individual? I mean, what the fuck is it, would you say, that makes alcohol so goddamn attractive?"

"Well," Tricia replied, still with her back to them, "that was certainly a mouthful. I suppose only writers can do that." And turning to them with the glasses of gin, and chancing a quick glance into the brown eyes, "It gets you drunk. Can't you just live with that?"

Margot took up the glass. "Nothing philosophical in that."

Tricia smiled at her, but with her eyes more than with her mouth. "Well, I guess, alcohol is like sex—just like sex. You drink it, you have an orgasm, and that's it."

Letting her eyes go closed for a moment, Margot said, "So, you see alcohol as both necessary and enjoyable?"

"Sure."

"So," said Shelly to Tricia, "would you say that it was God or the devil who gave alcohol to humanity?"

Taking her seat again and crossing her legs, as if to be modest about what was between them, "God, of course. Just as he is behind sex. I think God gave sex and alcohol to comfort the soul in pain. So, the question for us, who are in pain, is— would we rather experience intoxication or ecstasy."

"Talk about a mouthful," he returned. "Maybe you should write. You have wonderful diction and a seductive way of speaking."

Margot threw him an unhappy glance for this, but then asked Tricia, "Do you enjoy alcohol?"

"I do."

"Do you enjoy getting drunk?"

"Affirmative."

"Do you enjoy having sex?"

"Very much."

"Do you enjoy making business calculations?"

"I sure as fucking hell do."

"So," she concluded, "you must enjoy business more than sex or alcohol."

Tricia ran a hand down her leg, as if appreciating her own flesh. "Well," she replied, "I wouldn't want to live without any of them. But— desert island, and all that?—yes, I'd probably choose the accounting book."

"Would you say, then, that your soul is more in your mind than between your legs?"

Cocking her head, so that the hair fell over one lens of her glasses, she answered, "More, yes."

Shelly took a sip from his drink, then said, "I'd choose the alcohol."

Tricia smiled. "And which would Margot choose?"

Margot put her tongue between her lips, then answered, "The sex."

"It's funny," added Tricia, "how everybody's architecture is different, right?"

The three turned as Henney, in tweed pants, cashmere sweater, and bedroom slippers, entered from a side doorway. They continued to watch as she went to a window, turned down a blind, then came to the bar and took a seat. She had not put her hair up, so that now it lay draped, long and elegant, to her shoulders. As she obviously preferred a more natural look, the cosmetics had been kept to a minimum. The only exception was the lipstick, which had been meticulously applied, and whose color Shelly later described as an ungodly alizarin crimson.

"What's this," she queried happily, "lunch already?" And pointing to a greenish brown bottle of scotch, "Tricia, would you be able to get me one of those, on ice? But continue, ladies, please."

"Actually," said Tricia, pouring the drink, "we were just talking about sex and alcohol."

"And?"

"And nothing. Just—sex and alcohol." And placing the drink on the bar, "Here you go."

Henney took it, tipped it up and simply drank it down. When Tricia immediately reached for the bottle and refilled the glass, Henney took it up again, but this time merely held it, smiling around at them.

"All right," said Shelly, watching her, "here's a question for everybody, and it's always asked, so it's neutral. But it's usually asked in three's, like what three things would you take with you on a desert island. But let's do one. What's the one thing you would take with you? Tricia, how about you?"

Henney looked around at them, as if happy to be playing an interesting game. Lifting the glass to her nose, she smelled it, then took a sip of the whiskey.

Tricia, watching this, replied, "I have no idea, Shelly. Probably a long book of some kind, maybe about business. What would you take with you?"

He also took a sip of his gin. "My paintbox," he answered, "full of paint, of course. I think that's all I would need."

"Even if they didn't rescue you for twenty years?"

"Yes."

Margot cleared her throat. "I think, for myself, a typewriter and paper would do the trick."

Now all three looked at Henney, who sat contentedly smelling her whiskey.

But she merely smiled at them, then replied, "Oh, it's my turn, yes. Well, I'm sorry, but I would simply never be able to decide what to take. Should I take gin, or should I take scotch? Which is a realistic dilemma, right? I mean, who realistically would ever be able to decide between the two?"

Later, as they enjoyed a luscious lunch of chicken salad and white wine, by a window overlooking the pool, Henney pointed toward the river and complained, "Isn't it muddy, the river, in winter?"

"I don't see any mud, Bonnie," returned Tricia with an impatient sigh, "just water."

Henney took up her wine. "Well, maybe you're right. But it's Florida, for goodness' sake, which is practically the tropics. Everything spoils in the tropics."

"We could," offered Tricia, touching the bridge of her glasses, "move to Miami."

"Move the gallery? I hardly think so. ... Oh, and speaking of the gallery, I am happy to report, Shelly, Margot, our two stars, that we're planning a second show."

Both caught the slight roll of Tricia's eyes.

"The first," Henney continued, as if in soliloquy, "was so successful! And we have received numerous requests to have a second. Tricia thinks we should plan to have it around Easter. Isn't that right, Tricia?"

Reaching for her wine and with the glass just at her lips, and raising her eyebrows, "Yes. Easter would be, uh—yes, I did say that. Excellent. Why not?"

Henney turned to Shelly. "How does that sound?"

He blinked, then looked at Margot, as if for help. "I suppose, Bonnie," he answered. "Yes, sure. I'd love to do another show. Margot?"

Margot merely nodded.

"Oh," Henney continued, "and we're thinking of including about twice as many paintings. We can put some works on the floor this time. But do you think you can give us twice as many? In the same style, of course."

He shrugged. "I don't see why not."

"Well, do you have that many ready now?"

"No. But I will. I shouldn't have a problem with it."

"Excellent."

But Tricia, setting her glass down, gave Shelly a look. "You know what we're hoping, don't you?"

"Uh—no, I don't."

"We're hoping to get as many shows in as possible before some critic turns on you."

"Now, Tricia," put in Henney, "let's not be negative."

Giving her glasses a push, "All it takes is one, Bonnie, you know that, just one birdbrain critic in that goddamn Times Union of yours."

Henney put her fork down. "Okay, so now you are definitely being negative. What, you don't want to do another show?"

"Yes, Bonnie, I do. But I am getting the creeps about doing it at the gallery."

"Your alternative?"

With an unhappy shrug, "I don't know, maybe do it in Miami or Atlanta, then come back with another show here, say, next September."

Henney gave her a confused look. "But we had already talked about it, Tricia. Why are you saying this now?"

Tricia's eyes found Shelly's, then Margot's, then went to the wine glass. "I don't know, Bonnie. Modern art has that novelty element that can win somebody one day, yet bore them the next. We don't want to overload. I think we should control very carefully the number of S. Byrne paintings we release. If we don't do that, we'll sell quickly and make a lot of money. But then the collectors will get bored and the sales will stop. And then, like I said, some sadistic art critic will come in for the kill, write that his work's banal, and it will be all over."

Henney took up her wine again, held it thoughtfully, then simply drank it down. "Miami?" And after a single nod from Tricia, "All right, let me think about it for a minute or two here." And to Shelly, "I know my art, and I'm not wrong—I'm never wrong. But Tricia's got the smarts when it comes to the numbers, the odds, the market, the collectors. . . . Okay, let's try Miami, then. What do you say to that, ladies?"

Again, as if for help, Shelly looked across at Margot. He trusted her the way Henney trusted Tricia. "Well?" he queried.

Margot lifted her glass. "Makes sense, Shelly. Yeah—yeah, I think it makes sense."

He cleared his throat, then said, "I don't know the market. In fact, I don't know much about collectors or how they think or anything else about selling art. I just don't have a head for it—business, I mean. So, I agree. . . . But I feel a little compelled here to say something about my art—just for us here, since we're all in this together."

Henney raised her eyebrows. "Go ahead, we'd love to hear it."

"You both saw my work. I'm not consistent. I have an experimental side. And I'm not prepared to continue to paint in a certain style just because people expect it or even are asking for it. I love my current things, and I'll probably continue to paint them for practically ever, I guess. But I get bored, too. And I want to warn you, since your investment with the framing, the gallery, the advertising, and all the rest, is considerable—that I am not prepared to produce just to sell. I'm always looking for something new in my art, and I want to feel free to do that. So, what I'm saying, I guess, is that I'm going to paint what I want, and I'll take my chances with the future."

Henney smiled. "Actually Tricia and I both probably knew what you were going to say. You can set your mind at rest, Shelly, we're not about to put all our eggs, so to speak, in one artist. You have to be real, but we have to be realistic. Tricia's just talking about the marketing side, the selling part. But, yes, be yourself, of course. We expect it. You be yourself, and we'll tell you whether we can sell it or not."

Margot then said, "Bonnie, this has been a wonderful lunch. I hope you don't mind if I ask you—do you have a full-time chef?"

Henney blinked at the sudden change of subject, but then replied, "Well, of course I don't really cook. I never have. I'm sure Tricia can cook, she can do anything, but where would be the time? Her talents are so beyond such things anyway. But yes, a chef—a wonderful lady, very talented. She's here every day and evening. She's pretty and thin and swims like a fish, I can tell you. She doesn't do too much tasting of her own creations, if you know what I mean, but she does eat praise, and I can't blame her, she's so very talented. I will pass along your compliment."

CHAPTER 25

January 1962

The fact that her ex-husband lived a mere few blocks away continually played on Margot's mind and was beginning severely to affect not only the writing but the painting as well. Although she had not seen Joey since that early November day when he had asked for money, except for a couple of times around the neighborhood, she had seen Danny on his bike near Two Points. She had seen nothing of Joey's brother Bobby or his wife.

Nearly every day now she could see evidence of Shelly's anxiety, even in the way he walked, as if it was becoming an unbearable weight. For herself, not only the danger of a seemingly imminent attack of some kind from Joey, but also the guilt from her own procrastination in doing anything about it, had brought the writing to a near halt.

One day, while shopping at the food store near Avondale, she turned into his aisle as he was pulling a package of toilet paper from the shelf.

But when he saw her he quickly shoved the package back onto the shelf and began to push his cart again. She knew how he loathed to go to a supermarket, and could only imagine what menial chores his sister-in-law was making him do around the house.

"Hey, Joey," she said as she passed his cart, "she'll be mad if you don't go back and get the toilet paper. Has she got you running the vacuum cleaner too and maybe doing a few dishes?"

"Hey," he said somewhat angrily, "when am I going to see that money? You and your girlfriend had better just cough it up. I didn't say I needed it because I didn't need it, stupid—I said it 'cause I needed it."

"Oh, yeah? And how much do you need now, a million dollars?"

"Actually I only need a thousand. But I'd better see it soon, or you know what."

"No, I don't know what, Joey. Why don't you explain it to me again."

Momentarily, "How about five hundred?"

"No."

He stared at her. "How about two hundred, then?"

Here she turned and pushed her cart toward the toilet paper, where she pulled off a package and stuck it on top of her groceries. She knew he was watching her, so she turned and said to him, "We actually use toilet paper. I guess you wipe your ass with blackmail money."

At the checkout she pushed the cart into the line next to his, grabbed a magazine, and watched him. When he took a pack of chewing gum to add to his groceries, she said aloud, so that the others in line and the cashier could hear, "Hey! Are you stealing that pack of gum?"

Startled, he quickly put it back on the shelf. And glaring at her, "No, I'm not! Just shut up, would you?" But when she discreetly gave him the finger, then turned back to her magazine, he said, "How about a hundred? A hundred dollars, and I'll walk away, I swear to God."

Without looking at him, "No."

"Fifty? This is your last chance, and you can tell your kissin' cousin that, too."

Casually she flipped another page. "No."

As the line advanced she began putting her groceries onto the belt. Her back was to him, and she could feel his anger as he watched her.

"You're so cheap, Margot," he said, raising his voice, "you probably wouldn't even give me five goddamn bucks, would you?"

She stopped loading her groceries onto the belt. With everyone now looking at them, she slowly pulled her purse around, got her wallet and took out a dime. Turning to him, she took up the March of Dimes donation canister from the counter, dropped in the coin, and replied, "No." Replacing the canister, she turned back to her groceries.

For a moment he just stood there, glowering fiercely at her back. Then he looked around at everyone, including the cashiers, all of whom were staring at him. Suddenly he let out a loud croaking sound, grabbed his cart, flipped it over onto the floor, spilling out the groceries, then simply stomped from the store.

She did not turn to watch him leave, but said to the cashier, "I apologize. That man was stealing chewing gum, and I just had to say something. Gracious, what's this world coming to!"

She knew he would be waiting for her outside. Just before leaving she stopped at the door and reached into her purse to check the .38. There were tissues on it, so she stuffed them to the side, allowing the grip to stick up. Leaving the zipper open, she pushed the cart through the door and toward the car.

Not seeing him, she opened the passenger-side back door, grabbed a bag and put it in, then another, then the last. She shut the door, returned the cart to the sidewalk, then returned to the car, got in and lowered her window. Then she saw him, just beside the car in front of hers, walking toward her.

"Hey there!" he said sharply, now at her window, putting his arm up on the car. "Goin' home with all your groceries, huh? Think it's just that easy?"

Keeping her eyes on his face, she pulled the open purse closer, then replied, "Easy? Yeah, it's just that easy, Joey. I might run over somebody on the way home, but even that will be easy, especially if it's you. . . . Now get your goddamn arm off my fucking car."

Grinning, he withdrew the arm, but then casually put a hand on the fender. "You don't think anybody'll try to stop you, huh?"

"Get your hand off my fender. Your dirt will ruin the shine."

Leaving the hand there, he returned menacingly, "Ho, ho! It looks like it's been washed and waxed."

"It has," she replied. "But even shit will eat through Turtle Wax."

Lifting his hand from the car, he sneered at her. "I'm gonna give you a call some night. You can bet on that."

"Or," she returned, her hand hovering just above the grip of the .38, "you could have the courage to come around to the house. But then, you don't have the courage, do you, Joey? You send little Danny with a Halloween costume and a gun."

As he took a step back from the window she could see his face redden with anger and the vein bulge at his temple. With her hand now hard on the grip of the .38, and her finger on its trigger, she watched as he simply pointed at her with his finger, then turned and walked away. She followed him with her eyes until he got into a dark blue Pontiac, briefly sat staring at her, then started up and drove off.

Lifting her hand from the gun, she reached to adjust her rearview mirror, then caught her breath. In the mirror, but clearly, she saw him. Directly behind her car, in the opposite parking aisle, the man from the softball field, the camera oddly still slung around his neck, was putting a bag of groceries into the back seat of a white Bel Air. After shutting the door, he turned and looked toward her car for a moment. As he did she caught in the mirror the butt of a .45 automatic slung in a shoulder holster just inside his jacket. Then he simply got in, backed out, and drove away.

"Jesus!" she muttered. "He must have been in the store." Then she turned the key, pulled the shift down, backed out, and left the parking lot.

That evening, Margot looked up from unwrapping a typewriter ribbon. She did not need to ask, but did anyway. "Was that him on the phone?"

"It was. Margie, he threatened me." And folding his arms, "He said he was going to catch me out some night. What in the hell does that mean, Margie? Now, you haven't done anything about this, even though you said you would. He's your ex-husband."

Clearing her throat, "That's true. But he wants your money, too."

"But you haven't done anything, Margie! You've just sat and done nothing. You're the one that knows about these things, I'm not. God!"

"Actually I started doing something about it today. I saw him at the supermarket."

"What did you do?"

With a shrug, "I just said a few things to him."

"Well, what?"

"Just a few things I knew would make his blood pretty much boil."

Incredulous, "Why in God's name did you do that?"

"To get things moving, why do you think?"

"And that was wise?"

"Well, he called, didn't he?"

"You wanted him to? Why the hell did you want him to, Margie?"

She wadded up the package, then dropped it into the trash basket. Leaning back, then folding her arms, she answered, "Because you can't paint and I can't write, that's why."

Again he was incredulous. "And what am I supposed to do with that? I've been afraid even to go to the drugstore, and now I'll be afraid to go out of the house."

"So, don't. Just stay in."

Letting his arms drop, he stared at her helplessly. "I'm supposed to just stay at home? For how long?"

"Don't worry, Shelly, it probably won't be for long. I made him pretty mad."

"Well, I'm kind of mad myself—but at you!" And walking away, but then turning back, "And you can get the phone next time it rings. I'm just not answering it. Oh—yeah—and I've got a goddamn stomach ache!"

Momentarily, "I don't want to make your stomach ache worse, but when I saw Joey at the supermarket, I saw the man with the camera too. He must have been in the store when we were. And know what? He had been shopping and still had the camera around his neck. Why would he do that? Odd, right?"

CHAPTER 26

The next afternoon, while Shelly was in the shower, the phone rang. Margot pushed herself from the typewriter and took a deep breath. Going to the phone, she picked up the receiver and said hello. For a moment, she heard only silence, but then his voice.

"Last warning, Margot."

"You frightened Shelly, you dirty fucking prick. You shouldn't have done that."

"Shut up! I want the money. Oh, and it's the full two thousand now. And you can tell your pussy pal, if I don't get it, I'm catchin' one of yous out in the dark some night."

"All right, Joey," she returned, "I'll talk to him. Give me your number and I'll call you right back. He's in the bathroom, using our new toilet paper."

"Hey," he chuckled, "that's cute."

After writing the number down, she replaced the receiver, then lifted it again and dialed. "Hi, Joey. The answer's no. And you know what else? I say you're a coward, yellow to the goddamn bone. You sent your nephew around with a gun, because you were too afraid to come yourself. Little Danny in a Halloween costume, with a gun, because you were too afraid. You're such a coward you can't even buy toilet paper in a store. That's what you are, a tiny coward hiding behind little Danny. And you probably stole his candy when he got home. You're a little prissy sissy, Joey. Stealing candy from a child, you little coward. You're too afraid to come over here yourself, you little chickenshit! I'm a girl, and you're afraid of me, you little sissy." She waited for his response, but heard only his hot breathing. Then she said, "Not a dime, you filthy little coward prick! But if you're really hard up for toilet paper, since you're too namby-pamby to buy it in the store yourself, you can have some of ours. It's used, but it's good enough for a coward." Here she simply hung up and walked away from the phone.

After calling to Shelly to get out of the shower, she grabbed a box of ammunition from the kitchen cabinet and pulled its tray out. Taking up the pump from its place beside the counter, she chambered it, then flipped it over and slid in another of the big shells of double aught to fill the magazine.

Going up to the bathroom again, she threw the door open and commanded, "Come on, get dressed, and get yourself armed."

For a moment he simply stared at her, but then queried, "He called?"

Turning from him, "Yes. And I made him really, really mad. I burned him, Shelly. I know what to say to Joey Lucci, and I said it."

"And consequences, Margie?"

"Oh, there'll be consequences."

Later, with the sun going down, they went to the kitchen, made spaghetti, and opened a bottle of wine. It was an unusually mild winter evening, even for Florida. Shelly even left the kitchen door open to help clear the cooking smells.

As they sat with after-dinner tea Shelly queried, "Should I start carrying it around the house again?"

She put her cup down. "Yes, obviously."

"Now?"

"Yes. Get the holster out too, or just tote the gun in that purse you carry around here."

"You don't think we're being premature?"

"Shelly, he could come here tonight."

"So, I should actually be wearing the holster and gun right now?"

For a moment she said nothing, but simply took up her glass and finished the last few drops of her wine. Then she said, "I think I'm going to let you learn on the job. When he gets here, you decide what you want to do. But you should know—I deliberately made the bastard ex-cop Joey Lucci mad as fucking hell to get him to come over here and try to kill us. So, yeah, if you want to wait until he shows up to look for your gun, fine." Here she slipped her gun from the holster in her jeans, swung the cylinder out, closed it, then laid the piece on the table. Picking up her teacup, she took a sip, then said, "But I'm going to be ready."

"No," he returned quickly. "No, no, I got it, I understand, Margie, I was just making sure. I thought we'd done with all this stuff, after my dad. But here we are again, with people coming to our house to murder us. . . . I'm sorry. I wish I was stronger. I know running away is not any good. You were right, he came here because you signed on the alimony papers, and he'll follow us wherever we go. He's following the money, and he'll follow us for as long as it takes to get money out of us. And he'll hurt or kill us, if we don't give it to him. I know that—I know it. But the truth is—still is—I'm weak, not strong, and I'm afraid."

"Too bad," she replied. "I'm sorry. You were sorry for your dad, and now I'm sorry for my ex."

But he continued, "I was trying to paint this afternoon. It was on a draft. Great ideas. Beautiful. I put out the paint, softened it up, then mixed the colors all across the palette. I poured the oil, the varnish, the turp. Everything was so ready. But then, nothing came out of me, absolutely nothing. But I started anyway, smearing up to the right, down to the left, down and up the middle. I even tried to work in tiny areas with a smaller knife. Still nothing. Things got so muddied and ugly that I had to scrape off, turp the surface, and set it aside. All of it was a waste."

"Not part of the creative process, huh?"

"Obviously it wasn't. It was because of this bullshit." And hanging his head, "Look, I'll go and get my gun and holster out. It's fine. I'm just poor-mouthing the world, that's all. Should we start practicing again?"

"There probably won't be time for that. Besides, I think we're pretty good with these. You're a little timid with the 12-gauge, but you're fine with your .38."

"Can you blame me? That shotgun gave me a yellow arm, Margie. I couldn't paint for a week. No, the revolver's my protection, I'm fine with that."

"Well, we're sleeping with our protection tonight. We might shoot ourselves or each other, but we're going to be ready for this fucker."

"What about calling the police?"

"Oh yeah, we'll call them. But not yet. ... Listen, I'm going up to do some lifting and then take a shower. Make sure all the windows and doors are locked before you come up."

"So, you think he'll come tonight."

After a single blink, "Maybe, Shelly, yeah. But I'm going to drill him, if he does, I swear to God."

Momentarily, "I saw the man with the camera again—this afternoon. He was just sitting in a white car in the parking lot across the street. I think he was looking toward the house. After about an hour, he started up and drove off."

She looked toward the ceiling, then ran a hand through her hair. "Jesus! The whole world's after us. You know what? Let them come and get us, the goddamn people! And if that camera guy sticks a toe on this property, I might just drill him too."

"This might be the end of our work, Margie— your new book, my series for the Miami show."

With a shrug, "So what? I'm tired of all these threats. I'll write my book in blood, and you can paint your paintings in blood. Joey and his stupid brother. And that man with the camera, he'd better trade it in for a gun, because I'm going to shoot him too. Fuck the whole world! Now I'm going up, just like it was a regular evening. And I'm going to lift weights, and I'm going to take a shower, and then maybe I'll try to do some writing. After that, I'm going to get my usual snack and eat like I was a goddamn little kid, and get milk on my face. Then I'm going to get into bed and hopefully sleep. And I'd better not hear anybody out there touch a doorknob or a window."

And getting up, she went over to where the countertops met, bent down and retrieved the mousetrap she left there each night. Casually she held it over the trashcan, pulled the wire, and let the dead mouse fall. After resetting the trap, she set it back in its place and left the kitchen.

CHAPTER 27

They could not sleep. Together they listened for the remnants of the cold wind that had blown up from the St. Johns for much of the afternoon, but heard nothing. Outside a kind of stagnant chill surrounded the house.

"You know what bothers me the most right now?" queried Margot through the darkness. "It's not that these morons have disturbed my writing and my sleep, it's that they've disturbed me so much I can't even kiss my girl good night."

"That's bad," he said, reaching over to touch her shoulder. "Why don't you kiss me anyway?"

"I can't, I'm too upset."

"Well," he returned, slipping an arm over her stomach, "then I'll just have to kiss you." And he did. But when they turned away from each other and still could not sleep, he said, "Margie, I hear mice in the kitchen. The skittering bothers me. You set that trap again carefully?"

"Of course I did. I know my mousetraps."

"I think you should put out more traps."

"Tomorrow."

"Where's the shotgun, Margie?"

"You're saying my name too much. Since we're the only two in this bed, you don't actually need to use my name at all."

"Sorry, I'm a bit tense. I'm thinking I hear him at the window or out by the car or walking through the house."

Wearily, "The shotgun's beside me here. I've just left the safety on, so be careful with it, if you need it."

He reached for the handkerchief on his night table, then blew his nose. Pulling the covers back up to his chin, he tried to occupy himself by watching the spots of various outside lights as they flickered on the wallpaper. But none of this did him any good, so he said, "Margie, why don't we talk for awhile?"

She turned onto her back. "Sure. What about?"

"Let's ask each other questions. . . . Me first. Who's your favorite composer?"

She yawned, then answered, "Bruckner."

"Why?"

"Because he was so handsome. Who's yours?"

"Stravinsky," he returned, fighting a chuckle, "because he was so tall." But closing his eyes, "Laughing is good, but I'm not sure it will help me sleep."

"So," she continued, "why did Van Gogh cut off his ear?"

"Just part of the lobe, they think now. But I've never heard a good explanation of his motive. My guess is that it was simply an impulsive, frenetic act."

"An insane act?"

"Not at all. Probably just a cry to God for help."

"Sounds plausible."

"Why did Hemingway kill himself?"

"His wife says he was just cleaning his guns."

Sniffing, "Right. So, why?"

She closed her eyes, then looked up at the dark ceiling. "Well, I guess it was to cry out to God for help."

"Insane?"

"No," she answered. "No more than Van Gogh. I would think both were a little too sane for their own good. But Hemingway was a bit of an asshole, I think. Maybe he just got tired of wallowing in his tough-guy mentality."

"Sounds plausible. . . . Your turn."

"What's your favorite art movement?"

"Actually," he replied, "the Fauves, I think. What's your favorite literary movement?"

She took a moment, then answered, "For me, literary movements are hard to identify."

"Is life clear for you, Margie? Are you certain about things?"

"No and no. . . . What do you want out of life, Shelly?"

"I don't know. I suppose, just peace. What do you want out of life, Margie?"

"I don't know. Maybe love. . . . By the way, I love you. I want to say that, in case something bad happens to either you or me tonight."

"So, you think he'll come tonight?" But it was then that they both heard it, and he queried, "What was that?"

She sat up. Angrily she replied, "It's the gravel. Somebody's out by the car."

Getting out of bed, they pulled on their jeans, then stuffed their guns and extra ammo into their pockets. Margot reached for the shotgun, then whispered for him to stay just behind her.

"Let's grab a flashlight," he said.

Grimly, "No. It'll just give them something to shoot at." Then, gritting her teeth, "Besides, I want to make some mistakes tonight. Which means—I don't care if I can see who I'm killing, I'm just going to fucking kill him. Come on."

Entering the dark kitchen, they heard a mouse skitter away over paper. Suddenly there came the sound of glass being smashed just outside the kitchen door. Then another crash. Margot stepped to the window and watched as a dark figure swung again.

"He's smashing the car windows with a crowbar," she whispered. "See him? He's on the other side of the car now."

As yet another crash of glass sounded, Shelly replied, "I can't see a thing, Margie. Be careful."

"He's going to smash the windshield now. Get ready." Then a huge crash sounded as the windshield was beaten through. She put her arm back in the darkness, touched Shelly, and then pushed him away. "Get back," she said. "Watch this."

Raising the shotgun, she prepared to shoot through the kitchen door at the dark form beside the car. But just as she put her finger on the trigger there was a huge blast-flash from the gun of someone else in the driveway, then rapidly four more blasts. Pulling the shotgun up, she turned around to Shelly.

But Shelly had himself turned back to the doorway. "Someone's there, Margie," he blurted. "Someone's in the house!" But instantly a flash came, and he called out in pain and fell.

She did not look down at him, but trained her eyes on the doorway to the hall. Leaning the shotgun against the counter, she pulled instead the .38 from her pocket and with both hands brought it up in front of her. Then from the doorway she heard the eerie voice.

"It's me, bitch!"

And that was all she needed. Lunging forward, she fired six times at the area just below the voice—*Pop!-Pop!-Pop!-Pop!-Pop!-Pop!*" Then she swung the cylinder out, punched the empties free, pulled a handful of cartridges from her pocket, and reloaded. Reaching out for the switch, she flipped it up, and looked down at him. Stepping over his form, and with the gun on him, she grabbed his wrist and pulled him onto his back. Then, aiming down at his face, she said, "Go straight to hell, Joey," and pulled the trigger until the gun was empty.

"Margot!" called Shelly frantically from the kitchen floor. "Margot! There's another one out in the driveway!"

But even as Margot reloaded again there came a man's shout from just outside the kitchen door.

"Hey! Hey! Don't shoot! Everybody okay in there? I'm with the police. I got this one out here.

If you're okay, open the door slowly and show your face. It's okay, I'm with the police."

Quickly she switched the light back off. Without answering him, she bent over Shelly and queried, "Where'd he hit you?"

"In my leg!"

"Yeah, okay. Press on it, press hard. That's right." Then, gritting her teeth, she stood and walked to the kitchen door.

"Hey!" came the shout again. "Hey, in there! Everybody okay? Come on out, if you are."

Now she threw the latch, and pulled the inner door open. Gripping the .38, she said through the screen door, out into the darkness, "Tell you what, mother fucker, Joey's dead, and I'm going to kill you too if you put one goddamn finger on this door."

"Okay, okay, take it easy, ma'am, back off. I'm with the police. I'm going to go back to my car and put a call in. Take it easy, it's okay. Just stay there. . . . Oh, how's the other one?"

Blinking, she replied, "She's hurt."

"Okay, lady. Just stay there. I'll call."

"Fortunately," said Margot as she slipped coins into the Coke machine, "we live just down the street."

Detective Tipper nodded. "Yes. He probably wouldn't have bled to death, but still, it was good to get him here fast like that."

Retrieving the bottle, she inserted it and pulled it down to remove the cap. "So, you don't know where the other guy is?"

"Not right now, I don't. But he's with us, like he said. He's okay, he's fine. He just kind of keeps to himself."

She looked at the part in the combed, oily hair, then tipped the bottle up for a drink.

As if by the power of suggestion, he ran a hand over the top of his hair. "Listen, you need to come down to my office as soon as you can. I mean, make sure Mr. Byrne's okay first, of course. But we need to talk. I know you gave the cops a full report, but I'd like to ask you a few questions myself, if you don't mind."

"Is there going to be a problem?"

He shook his head and looked down. "No. He was in your house. You could have shot him even if he didn't have a gun. But I do want to talk. Is that okay?"

"Sure. I'll call for an appointment."

He put his hat on and smiled at her. "You won't need an appointment. . . . Oh, I might be out, so you'd better call just to make sure I'm there."

She looked at him, thinking how it was necessary for the silk hatband to ride up next to his oily hair, so that the hat could decorate his head and protect his brain. "All right," she replied, "I'll call, then."

Three days later Shelly sat in his wheelchair in the living room and looked around at the paintings. He could hear the kitchen doors being closed tight as Margot brought in the bag and crutches from the car. Wheeling himself toward the kitchen, he winced as an electric shock-like pain ran down his leg. The thigh bone had been chipped by the bullet, which had passed all the way through the leg. The pain, however, which the surgeon said would increase, had at times become so intense that he was forced to take the codeine.

"Goddammit, this thing hurts!" he uttered as Margot put the kettle on to boil.

The other pushed her bangs aside, then replied, "Well, you were shot. Just be glad you're alive."

"What did Bonnie say?"

"She seemed pretty upset. She said it was a miracle your painting hand wasn't damaged. She said to give you their sympathy and tell you that you are in their prayers."

"That was nice."

"Well, knowing those two, I'm sure they'll soon be here for a visit. Bonnie even said she would love to have a peek at anything new you had finished and signed. Coming from anybody else, that would have been pretty crass. But not from her."

Giving his leg a quick rub, "It doesn't matter."

"Look, don't get negative on me. We're alive here. And we're ready to paint and write, with no more threats on our life, hopefully. So, don't get negative."

"Well, it hurts. And the doctor said it was going to get worse. So, if I complain a little bit, just take it, okay? Did you bring in the medicine?"

Shutting the kettle down, "I did."

"I'm going to need it—in a couple of minutes maybe. Damn, this hurts! What a bastard that Joey was."

Dropping teabags into cups, then pouring the cups full and setting them on the table, "Well, your dad was quite a bastard in his time, too. But we saw them both leave this world, so let's just try to get on with things. We have money and some success. We have to get you better and can't let this stuff get us down. We need to get back to work."

CHAPTER 28

After wheeling the Olds into the parking space, then pulling the key from the ignition, Margot sat for a moment, as if to savor the peacefulness of just being alone behind all the new glass. Then she dropped the keys into her purse and got out. Fortunately the dealer had been able to make all the repairs in only two days. Running a gloved hand over a fender, she closed her eyes and imagined how Joey's brother had smashed in most of the car's glass.

"Detective Tipper, please," she said at the desk. But instead of being asked to wait, she was immediately escorted by the sergeant to Tipper's office.

"Hello, Miss Bernard, please come in," Tipper said as she entered. "Please have a seat. Can I turn the fan on, or would you prefer it off?"

Choking a little from the residue of cigarette smoke and taking her seat, "Oh, maybe on. Shelly says to say hi."

He switched on the fan and twisted the screw on the arm at its back to make it oscillate. Even before taking his seat he began to look at her, as if somehow to reconsider something about her. Reaching for a pencil to hold, he queried, "Is that blowing on you too much? I can adjust it."

"No, no, it's fine, thanks."

"Yeah, I know," he chuckled. "It's probably hard for you to breathe in here—my wife says the same thing, God bless her. She sends me out on the back porch to smoke. Smoking's a bad habit. Lot's of people are quitting, but I can't seem to. I think it's just the stress of the job. . . . How is Mr. Byrne?"

She took her eyes from the oiled hair. "He's fine. He still has a lot of pain, but his leg seems to be healing well."

"Is he taking anything for it?"

"Yes, he has a strong prescription from the surgeon. I think the real problem for him will be the long convalescence necessary for healing the chipped bone. But he's an artist, and will still, I'm sure, be able to sit and paint. Nothing could keep him from that."

Momentarily he asked, "Do you have any questions for me, Miss Bernard?"

Hesitantly, "I guess I was expecting you to be asking me the questions, since I'm the one that shot him."

"Your ex-husband," he added. "Uh—I'm afraid that part is pretty simple. As I said before, he was in your house, and with a gun, and shot one of you before you shot at him. Actually there won't even be a hearing. You've been totally exonerated in what you did. Clearly the man had come to kill you—both of you."

"Don't you care why?"

"No."

"But what if I lured him there for some reason, then shot him?"

He gave a quick shrug.

"But—"

Raising a hand, as a traffic cop would do, "Stop, please, Miss Bernard. Really it doesn't matter. I don't care why you shot him."

Now she stared at him, making no attempt to hide her perplexity.

"I know you're probably worried," he said, "that I'm going to ask you about the extra six bullet holes in his face. I'm not going to ask you, don't worry. I don't care about the extra holes or why you obviously turned him over and then deliberately put them there. I will trust that you put them there for a good reason."

"So, why did you want to talk to me?"

He returned the pencil to the holder. "Well, for one thing, I wanted you to meet the man who killed the brother, Robert Lucci. Mr. Lucci was obviously trying to lure one or both of you outside to kill you."

"I—I certainly would like to meet him. I still don't know what he looks like, since it was all very dark."

"Yes. He said, by the way, that when you threatened to kill him, he took you very seriously and wouldn't have, in his own words, put a finger on that door for anything."

She smiled. "He was wise."

"Just a minute." And putting the desk phone's receiver to his ear, "Sergeant, could you please send in Mr. Pinkertt? . . . Thank you."

Soon there came a tap at the door and the man entered and stood looking at her, a simple smile on his face. She stared at him—the hat, the glasses, the familiar jacket, the slung camera. "Jesus!" she uttered softly. "You're kidding."

Then she stood and extended her hand. "I almost shot you," she said. "My apologies."

Meekly he shook her hand. "Well, you did nearly scare me to death, ma'am. After your warning, I wouldn't have touched that door."

"But, thank you," she said. "You probably saved our lives."

"I don't know, lady. If I hadn't been there, I think you would have just dispatched both of them. . . . Well, have to run. But it was nice meeting you. Sorry about Mr. Byrne. Someday we'll meet. Give him my best."

When Pinkertt had gone, Tipper returned to his chair and reached for another pencil. "He had been shadowing you and Mr. Byrne since the first man came to your house. When we're swamped, or just can't do anything further on a case, we often send him out to keep an eye on things. . . . Of course, as you can appreciate, he's practically the whole goddamn Marine Corps with a .45 automatic—please excuse the French. But yeah, you almost shot the best man I've ever seen with a gun."

"Sorry. It seems I almost shot an angel."

With a chuckle, "Yes, right, a guardian angel. Yes, that's very good. I'll have to tell him you said that."

"What about Robert's wife and Danny?"

"Don't worry about them," he replied. "I told her to count herself lucky not to be charged as an accomplice. I told her to get herself a job and a new man and to take care of her son. . . . She didn't argue."

Inadvertently her eyes went to the part in the hair. "Why are you doing this for us?"

"Well, I'll answer that," he said, "but first I have a question for you. And it's not rhetorical."

"Sure."

"How can you be so brutal and yet sensitive at the same time? I mean, it fascinates me. You overcome an armed killer with a baseball bat—"

"Softball."

Another chuckle. "Yes, right. But you overcome him and then beat him to death. And then you shoot an ex-policeman in the dark, hitting him squarely in the chest with all six shots. Then you reload and shoot him six times in the face. And yet your books—uh, well, let me just ask you that. How can you be so brutal and sensitive at the same time?"

"I have no idea, Mr. Tipper."

"James," he offered. "Or just make it Jim."

"Okay—*Jim*. And please call me Margot. But I have no idea how I can be that way. I guess, because it's not something I think about, it's just who I am. I write my books, because it's something I have to do, maybe just to get said what I think should be said. As to my brutal side, as you say, well, again, I suppose it's just part of the way I'm made. . . . And, my question to you?"

"Right. Well, just push that door closed, would you? . . . Right." Here he took out his wallet, extracted a photograph, turned it around on the blotter, then pushed it toward her. And when she had picked it up, "That's my daughter. Her name is Molly. She's the one in college, the one I was telling you and Mr. Byrne about."

"She's a doll."

"Yes. Well, uh, a little while back she attempted to take her own life. While she was in the hospital one of the counselors gave her your book. Now, forgive me for going on, but she's kind of mixed up, like I said. But she read your book—the one where the man puts on women's clothes and goes to the party—whatever it was, I don't know, I didn't actually read the whole book. But when I was talking with her there in the hospital she said just the fact that you had written about that kind of thing—and you understand, she's got something like that, which is why she attempted suicide—just your writing about it helped her. She looked me in the face and said, 'Daddy, I no longer want to kill myself. I see from this book that I can be who I am, and that I not only have meaning, but must have meaning'. . . . Miss Bernard, miss pretty lady with muscles, you saved my daughter's life. And when you saved her life, you saved my wife's life, and mine. . . . So, you ask me why I'm so much on your side? Frankly, you could have just walked over to that man's house and gunned him down in front of his TV set, and I'd have gotten you out of it. . . . Have I answered your question?"

With her eyes beginning to fill with tears, she answered softly, "Yes."

He watched as she opened her purse, took out a tissue, and dried her eyes. Then he simply stood and said, "All right, well—Margot—I've got a bit of a problem case out there I've got to go and take a look at." And giving her a hug, "Please give my greetings to Mr.—uh—to Shelly. And you go in peace. God bless! I'll see you around. Oh, and if you see Mr. Pinkertt around, don't shoot him—he's with us."

CHAPTER 29

Henney lowered her glass. "Well, you two are certainly getting yourselves a reputation," she said, "both in the arts and out."

From her barstool, Tricia, crossing her legs and cocking her head, added, "Yes, the next time art and literature take a plunge, you both could simply go to work for the police, since the crime-and-punishment thing always seems to be popular."

Margot merely smiled, her eyes going to Tricia's legs. Why would anyone walk around in winter in such a short skirt and bare legs, she thought, unless to invite the sensual desires of others? And just what was it with this woman? Such a piece of ass! But who's piece of ass was she? Or did she simply content herself with her own particular syndrome of parading her gorgeous ass so that the whole goddamn world might drool over it?

Then Henney queried, "Shelly, are you comfortable? You seem to be in pain."

From the over-pillowed chair, he answered, "I'm fine, thanks. Besides, alcohol fixes everything."

"And do you think you could handle being on the police force?"

He reached to adjust a pillow. "No," he replied, "but Margot could. Detective Tipper said that if it wasn't for her writing, which he certainly hoped she would continue with, he'd send her out in a squad car right now. He said if she ran out of bullets, she could just use a softball bat."

Chuckling, Tricia said, "I've never even fired a gun. I wouldn't know how to use one, even if I needed it. I suppose I would have to use a bat."

Henney, taking her eyes from Margot's arms, said, "I have fired a gun, and own one now. It was my husband's. I don't know why, but I just feel safer with it around. I even sleep with the thing. My husband used to shoot. He hunted birds with a shotgun. He'd go all over the world on excursions simply to hunt birds. I have wondered why anyone would ever want to shoot a bird. And even if they did, how could anything like that become at all popular? I can understand why shooting people might become popular. But birds? It doesn't make sense."

"It was good of the newspaper," said Shelly, adjusting the pillow under his leg, "not to play up the twelve bullet holes found in the body."

Tricia nodded. "Maybe you both have a friend in the police department who kept the story down."

"Yes," agreed Henney. "And what a story it could have been, with all the details that actually made it to the newspaper. What I read was like in a novel. There are usually, I think, only six shots in a gun. I know there are only six shots in mine. So, you must have reloaded."

"I did," said Margot. "I wasn't sure how many times I'd hit him, as dark as it was and as fast as everything was happening. So, I reloaded and fired again, yes."

"But, six in the chest and six in the face, with no misses, all in the dark, I assume—well, that's remarkable. Besides, he must have been down for the second group of shots."

Margot stopped flexing her muscles. For a moment she said nothing, wondering why the woman seemed to be backing her into this corner. Then she reached into her purse and extracted the hand squeezer she used when her concentration seemed to break up at writing. Slowly she began to squeeze the device with one hand. "Uh, yes," she replied, "he was down. But I'm sure people some-times shoot back even after they're down. Not being an expert in these things, of course, I simply fired away." Then shifting the device to the other hand, "It all happened so fast. And it was just pitch really. I couldn't see a thing."

Henney, who had been inhaling the vapors from her gin, lowered the glass. "I understand, yes. But still, that was remarkable shooting. Maybe you've got a talent for shooting, like a sniper has."

"And maybe," added Tricia, with an eye twinkle that showed even through the thick lenses, "you've also got a talent for shooting people, like an assassin has."

Margot looked at them, then replied, "Just lucky, I think. I'm not an expert."

"Wyatt Earp," said Tricia, "could both shoot and kill, no problem. Are you sure you're not like that?"

Margot cleared her throat. "No, I'm not like that. I'm not a killer, I'm a writer."

Henney tipped the glass up, then swallowed thoughtfully. "And why, Shelly, were you shot in the leg? You said you were standing."

"I was, yes," he said.

"But isn't that an odd place for an ex-policeman to shoot someone? Wouldn't he try for the upper part of your body? I mean, instinctively as well as by his training?" And when neither Shelly nor Margot responded to this, but merely took up their drinks, she suggested, "Perhaps he wasn't trying to actually kill either of you. Is that a possibility, do you think?"

Margot cocked her head. "I'm sure that's possible. Lots of things are possible. I really believe he intended to kill at least me, and I don't think it would have made sense for him to kill just me."

"But since it was dark, maybe he thought Shelly was you, and so really just tried to wound you."

"He knew it was Shelly, because Shelly had just said that someone was in the house, and then he knew it was me, because he said, 'It's me, bitch.' But who knows what was going through his mind exactly? Oh, and even a shot to the leg can easily be fatal. I mean, I'm not an expert, but the surgeon said Shelly could possibly have died."

"Oh, I'm sure he could have. I'm not saying, Margot, you shouldn't have done what you did. If someone's outside smashing up your car, and then another man comes into your house and starts shooting, you have no choice but to assume he's there to kill you. Which you rightly did—good for you. And you're such a good shot!"

"Just like Wyatt Earp," chimed Tricia, tilting her glass toward Margot.

Margot raised her glass to her lips. "Well—I'm not an expert."

"I'm sure you're not," said Henney. "But you're so quick thinking! Good for you."

"Well," said Shelly, a benevolent smile on his face, "like Margot said, we were lucky. Aren't you glad we were lucky, Margie?"

"But," said Henney, without waiting for Margot's reply, "I agree that it's good the newspaper didn't blow it out of proportion the way they usually do. They can crucify you." Then, peering into her glass, she added, "Which of course would make it more difficult to sell your paintings and books to the public."

"We're just happy," he said, "to be in the arts, to have a life in the arts. Margot and I are harmless people and just want to be left alone."

Suddenly Tricia, as if to announce that she was bored, slid from the stool, snatched up the bottle of gin, walked over to Henney, and without asking, simply poured alcohol down into the glass as the other held it. When Tricia queried whether anyone else wished a refresher, Henney said she did not want to overdo it before dinner. "But," replied,

Tricia, clearly exasperated, "I just poured yours, Bonnie, didn't you see that?"

Henney, blinking, looked into her glass. "Oh yes, of course. Thank you, Tricia, I'm all set. Perfect." Then, as Tricia refreshed her own drink and returned to the stool, Henney got up and went to the window. "What does everyone think," she queried, "should I have the pool enclosed and heated, or not? It would be splendid to take our drinks out there right now, sit on heated chairs, and have our dinner and wine brought out. Then we could just swim at our leisure for as long as we wanted. We could have cocktails and a few nuts or pieces of cake or some such. After that we could have a late-night martini and some cheese and crackers and, of course, olives. Wouldn't that be refreshing? What does everyone think?"

Tricia cleared her throat delicately. "That would, of course, be marvelous, Bonnie. Shall I call for estimates or just order it done?"

Still looking out the window, "I'm not sure. Do what you think is best, Tricia. I'm not versed in such things, as you know. You decide." Then taking to her chair again, "But would that suit everyone?"

"But," said Tricia, "the cost would be enormous, I should think."

"Would it?"

Tricia looked at Margot, then at Shelly, then replied, "Of course, Bonnie. You're talking about one fucking hell of a pile of gold to do something like that."

Somewhat startled, "Okay, sure, Tricia, I understand. What would it be—hundreds, or what? It's fine."

"No-o," returned Tricia, slowly shaking her head. "Try thousands and thousands. Lots of thousands, Bonnie."

Henney returned to her seat. "Well, that's fine, then. Just have it done. How long would it take, do you think?"

Giving the bridge of her glasses a nudge, "Uh— probably a couple of months at least. Is that all right? Shall I still try to get it done soon?"

"Yes, certainly before the summer, I would think."

With a roll of her eyes, Tricia looked at Shelly, then at Margot, then replied, "It's still January, Bonnie. So, we're not talking summer, more like spring."

"You mean, Easter?"

Nodding, "Right."

"But soon—so we can have our drinks out there. And it will all be heated? And the chairs too?"

Tricia let her eyes go closed, then returned, "Yes, Bonnie. That's what you said. Of course, sure. ... I'll make some calls tomorrow to get things started."

Henney made a sweep with her free arm. "And why do we not have music this evening? Is the piano player around?"

Frustrated, Tricia gave her glass a little push. "I could put a few of your favorite records on the new stereo, if you want. It sounds really great, Bonnie."

"Yes. What did we do with that?"

"You said to put it in one of the guest rooms, with the television set. ... Or I could give the pianist a call to see if she could come over and play for us now."

"Could you call her? I'd like to hear a few nice songs this evening. What does everyone think? Music? And we'll take our drinks out to the pool."

When Margot and Shelly simply shrugged, as if confused, Tricia said, "Let's wait until the enclosure's built, Bonnie. It's cold as hell out there now, and I'm not going out in my coat and sit around a goddamn pool when I can drink in here, okay?"

"But you like the pool."

Snatching up the drink and sliding from the stool, "Yeah, Bonnie, in the summer, when I can swim naked and drunk. But it's winter. There's nothing out there. It's cold, which is why we're talking about the enclosure and the heating and all the rest of it. You're the one that's been talking about it, for God's sake."

"Yes, of course. I understand that. That'll be fine."

With a sigh, "So, do you want me to call her or not?"

Henney got up and went to the window again. Looking out toward the pool, she replied, "Certainly. That would be very nice. Oh, and could you ask her if she could wear the same dress she wore for the party, when I announced Shelly's show? That would be very nice. ... That was a lovely evening, wasn't it?"